Heavy Whipped Cream

Mahogany B. Preston

ISBN: 978-1-959253-27-3

First printing, 2024 by Mahogany B. Preston

Trigger Warnings
Strong language
Adult situations
Alcohol Use
Taboo Relationship
Outdoor Intimacy

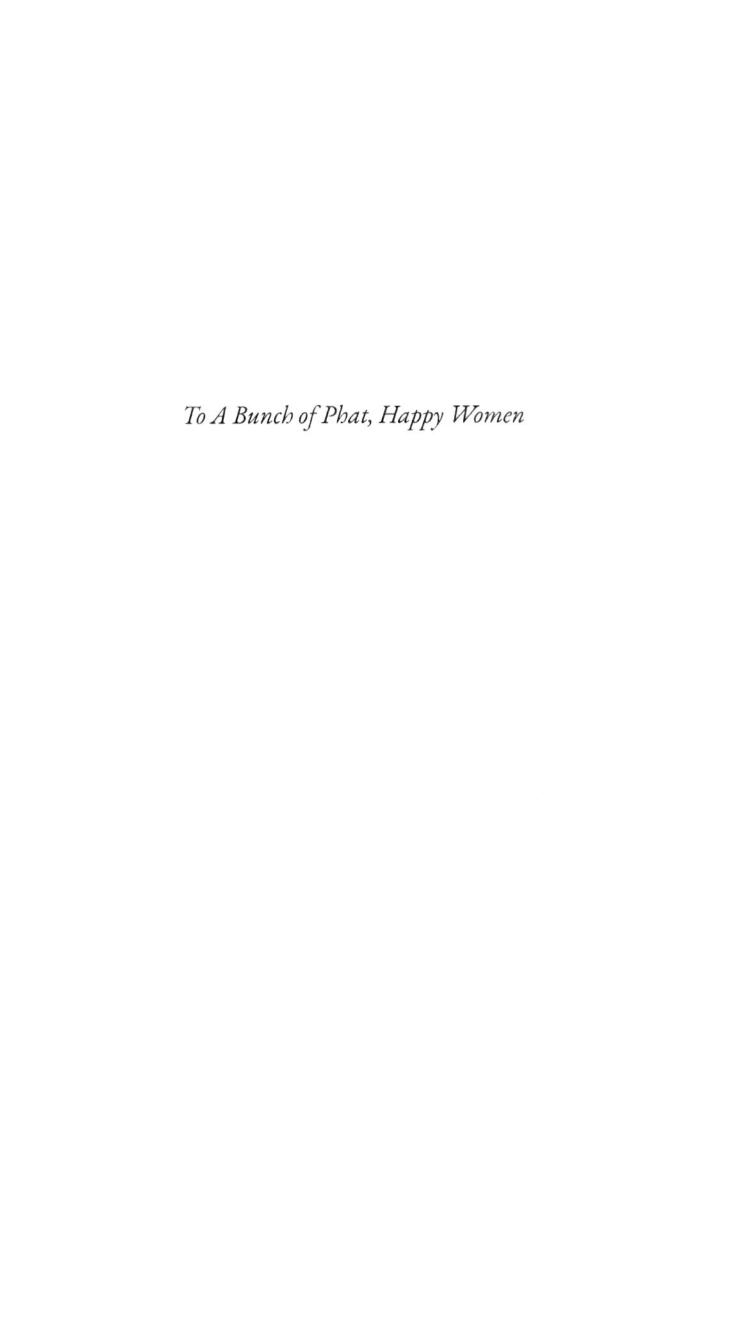

To A Bunch of Phat, Happy Women

Real men don't like skinny women. They only think they do because they're supposed to look better in clothes. But what happens when the clothes come off, and you climb between the sheets on a cold winter's night. Then they like to know they're with a real woman.

— Edna O'Brien

NOTE

This story is featured primarily in South Carolina. Language within the dialogue that is used by some of the characters feature the local (Geechee/Gullah) dialect, known in the surrounding Charleston areas. Please enjoy what is shared of the culture. Prepare yourself for some laugh out loud moments, pearl clutching moments, and a major I Know You Are F*cking Lying Moment.

MBP

CHAPTER 1

MIMI

While the scent of last night's indulgence seeps through his pores, I try to remember his name.

Coop? Maine? Something like that.

I struggle deciphering which one it is as I study the ridges of his abdomen above the line where the sheets cover his lower body. They look firm in the dim light bouncing from the television. Completely opposite where my hand rests across my stomach.

His high, brown cheekbones remind me of the teenage heartthrob back in high school all the girls fought over. All the girls—minus myself because girls who looked like me weren't on the radar of most boys back then. They loved petite frames, big asses, and slim waistlines. I had the ass—way more than I needed at that age—but also the mid-section to match.

Boys were either intimidated by my presence, lost in the many jiggles of my body when I walked past, or simply not attracted to me. But I was frequently told I had a nice set of lips, and Sonya, my big sister, warned me to stay away from any man that said those words to me.

His mouth resembles that of a male model you see on campaign ads. Full and pouty. As I try to remember what it felt like kissing them hours ago, I scour the room for my clothes he ripped off.

He's sound asleep and doesn't move while I writhe about. Either his alcoholic consumption has him under the spell of one too many whiskeys taken to the head, or the hours I've allowed him…I'm gonna call him Black Coffee…to cater to my never-tiring need has worn him out like a light.

My feet slip into my heels as I quietly button my dress. I grab my undergarments and slowly open the heavy door of the room without looking back. There's no time. A cab is waiting on me beyond the turnstile door, and I leave the hotel in haste with no regrets.

I bathe the night's muck from my skin—smoke, liquored kisses, and moisture from what's his name—then join my sister and mother at the breakfast table, mindful of their stares.

"You know, one-night stands weren't as risky in my day." Ma looks at me from behind her mug.

Sonya snickers, reaching for the paper at the edge of the table. "I warned you."

"Or told." I raise my brow.

"Your sister didn't have to tell me nothing, Mimi. I heard her come in three hours before you came strolling in with your heels tapping on my floor like a dancing horse."

"Well, Ma, I apologize for waking you up."

"Mm-hmm. You can repent at church. I'm gonna go finish getting dressed."

"I'm actually getting ready to hit the road. I have an early meeting in the morning and a lot to do."

Ma grunts. "Imagine that. I raised a daughter who came home for demon time but no time for Jesus."

"Ma, please."

"You can make that skip-and-a-hop drive after service."

I kiss her cheek. "I promise I'll go to church with you the next time I come home. I'll call you tonight."

Sonya carries my lightest bag to the car, dressed in her Sunday best.

"So, how was it?" she asks.

"From what I remember, pretty decent."

"Decent enough you're gonna see him again?"

"God no. I gave that fool a fake name and a fake number last night. I'm not looking for anything serious. You know that."

"Here we go again." Sonya sucks her teeth. "I know when you're lying. You enjoyed yourself."

"And so what if I did?"

"Mimi, you're gonna have to open up that heart of yours one day. And you better do it before this playgirl persona causes you to miss out on a real one."

"Girl, please. I ain't thinking about no one man. I'm thinking about two, three, and four of 'em." I chuckle.

"Yeah. Okay. Keep telling yourself that."

I hold her shoulder. "Pray for me today."

"I always do." We kiss each other's cheek. "It's probably a good thing *you'n* going with us to church. I'd hate to see my lil' sis burst into flames."

The reflex in my hand shoves her arm from much practice. "Hardy har har. Just because you're secretive doesn't mean you're innocent."

I crank my car and lower the window. Sonya starts gyrating in her Sunday best on the sidewalk to Lil Ru.

We sing along to the local classic.

"This here is a nasty songgggggg."

Mama steps out on the porch, and I turn the radio off.

Sonya laughs. "Go head home with your theme music."

I wave to the both of them. "Love ya, bye."

During the drive back to my apartment in Forest

Acres, my mind attempts to recreate my lover's face. It's impossible, thanks to my meeting him at a drunken hour and in a night club of flashing lights and clouds of smoke.

I faintly remember him as a whole, and by the time I make it home, he and the night become a memory, and my mind focuses on my presentation I'm due to give in the morning. Cheers to the weekend.

Chapter 2

COOP

Chatter and whispers rumble across the auditorium. The CEO has asked that all staff members congregate five minutes past nine for an important announcement.

It's a rare occurrence, and the majority of my colleagues are flushed with big, wide, panicky eyes. Worry covers nearly every face standing against the wall behind the back row, and Donald, my office neighbor and work buddy, twitches with impatience.

"If it were about bonuses, we would have received an email, so this must be big," says Donald, sighing impatiently while the late-comers search for a seat.

"I think you're right. I'm a tad nervous, to be honest. We're bombarded with email after email with nonsense every day, so why the spontaneous assembly?"

"Exactly my point. This news has to be huge. I smell layoffs."

The general manager of operations taps the microphone and quiets the room. The chatter dwindles to complete silence, and he thanks everyone for attending then announces the CEO to the stage.

Not a soul claps for her as she approaches the center. Light mutters resound before she speaks and clears her throat.

"Good morning," Mrs. Blackwell greets us. "I'm sure you all are wondering why I asked you to gather here this morning, so I'll get right to it. For quite some time, there has been talk of closing our Columbia branch. As of this morning, the company has decided to move forward with those plans."

Chatter builds in the room.

Mrs. Blackwell sighs into the microphone and raises her hand. "I, too, feel for those families and the shock of this sudden change. However, we were able to make some necessary changes within the company, and fortunately, a third of those employees will transfer here to the Summerville and Charleston corporate offices."

A hand raises near the front of the stage. "Are these transfers replacing us?"

Whispers crescendo in the room.

"I understand change isn't easy. And as of right now, no. The employees transferring to the Lowcountry are not replacing you. I called this meeting to inform you the offices will be restructured to accommodate the incoming employees, which means your cubicle space will more than likely be a tad smaller than you're used to. I ask that those of you who are asked to train or host a shadow show our incoming team hospitality and demonstrate what great leaders you are."

Donald grumbles. "I better not be training my replacement. I don't trust it, man."

A second hand goes up. "When will these transfers arrive, and when will our offices be remodeled?"

"None of you will be affected by the remodel. It begins tonight, and your colleagues will begin to trickle in over the next couple of weeks."

"Yeah, in a few weeks once they've decided to give us a pink slip." Donald sucks his teeth. "Guess I'll start looking at the want ads during lunch."

"Chill, bro. You're getting ahead of yourself."

"Why are you optimistic about all of this?"

"Because if I get to divide my workload in half, I'll be able to free up more weekends and enjoy the night life."

"Mind you, this influx of transfers might free up *every* weekend if the company is secretly replacing us." Donald breathes heavily from his nose. "Can never get too comfortable, my boy. Layoffs have been happening too often and too frequent to feel safe. All it takes is for one overachiever to come along, and you'll find yourself on the chopping block."

"I didn't think of it like that."

"What's with you today? You're all spaced out and more optimistic than usual. What do you know that I don't know?"

I smile and keep quiet.

CHAPTER 3

MIMI

"There's no way in hell I'm moving back into my mother's house."

Sage's eyes come alive. "Good, because I was gonna ask if you wanna bank the moving stipend and be roommates."

"I'd love to save some extra money a month on rent, but with the way I get down, it might ruin our friendship. It has before."

"How so?"

"Drama with my parade of men coming and going was the complaint. I don't wanna risk our friendship over no man. Sorry, friend."

Sage turns up her lip. "Well, there goes my plan A."

"Which was?"

"Cut costs as roomies, save the cash, and finally buy a house."

"And what was plan B?"

"I didn't have one. The rent is so high down in Charleston that I'll probably find a place way out in the outskirts."

"Tell you what. We can go looking together since I know the area better than you."

"I guess." Sage sighs. "You know what. Sorry I

asked about the roommate thing, because if I'm not feeling your neck of the woods, I'm not staying down there."

"We do have our own vibe in The Chuck, just like any other city, but I totally understand."

"And what vibe is that?"

I snicker. "You'll see soon enough."

The gentrification efforts of downtown have vastly changed the city from when I was a youth. While giving Sage a tour of places I enjoyed in my youth, but now they no longer exist, I feel like a stranger, a pretender in a sense, as I tell her stories about landmarks that have been torn down, renamed, and replaced.

"That place used to be called Coins. At least that's what we called it when I was growing up." I point to a corner store where we'd meet boys and watch old heads stand outside and sip beer in brown paper bags." I drive through a flashing light then stop at a red one two blocks up and feel dumbfounded. "There used to be a dry cleaner on that corner and a laundromat here," I tell her, looking at a mom-and-pop convenience store. "This is all new. When I come home to go out with my sister, we don't drive around this part of town. It never dawned on me how far the gentrification would spread. Jesus. I grew up in this area, and it doesn't even feel like home anymore."

"We just passed a laundromat. Look." Sage points to a new one built yards away from where the old one used to sit.

"That wasn't there back in the day. My mother used to drop us off where this building sits to do laundry. I'll never forget it because it was the place where my friends and I used to meet and dance in the parking lot while our clothes dried. It's also where my mother called me a smart-ass because one time I loaded all of our clothes in each dryer so it would take less time to finish, and she was mad as hell she had to turn around and pick us up as soon as she dropped us off." I giggle to myself.

Sage jokes. "Mrs. Reid needed a break from *y'all's* ass."

I nod. "I'm sure she did."

We browse in a few stores down on King Street and skip going to The Market to apartment hunt in Summerville before the offices close. The area has grown over the years and is the perfect distance away from my mother's house, West of the Ashley.

We settle for a new village built near the interstate in an area now called Nexton in Summerville—also easily accessible to the corporate office.

Sage looks at me like I'm crazy when I continuously say, "It's convenient and right by the I."

"Why do you keep saying that? The I. Is that what y'all call the highway?"

"Habit." I grin. "You know professional me. But when I'm home, what's ingrained in my roots always comes out."

"I peeped that hours ago. That accent of yours was thick when you took me downtown."

I shrug my shoulders. "It'll get worse when Sonya comes around."

"Can't wait to finally meet her."

Chapter 4

COOP

The parking lot is fuller than normal, which means the new people are piling in. I find a spot in the middle of the lot, saving myself a long walk when it's time to clock out and avoiding beads of sweat dripping down my face before the day even begins.

The Carolina sun will bake you like an unbasted turkey if you don't protect yourself, and already at eight o'clock in the morning, the temperature is approaching ninety degrees—not a good mix for a long-sleeve shirt and slacks.

Once I'm in the building, I keep my head straight, scouring the new faces on the sly, wondering which one will I have to work with directly—or let Donald tell it, is here to take my job.

The presence of new blood has shifted the energy in the building. Where you'd normally hear phones ringing and light banter between the cubicles and in the halls, the office is rather quiet, and you can feel intensity swirling in the air.

"Mr. Cooper." My supervisor, Mr. Findlay, taps on my open door. "How ya doing this morning?"

"Pretty good. How about yourself?"

"You know, the usual. Busy, busy, meetings, meetings. Same old, same old. Speaking of meetings, a few of the transfers haven't finished wrapping things up in the capital, so we've set up a Zoom call this morning to go over the details with a few of the team that will be working on our two biggest projects. I know it's last minute, but we need you in the room to go over the Craig Steele Development and a few other items."

"Sure thing."

"Great. See you in conference room G in ten."

After quickly checking my email, I grab a pen, my laptop, and a sticky pad. I can't help but stare at the new faces spread out across the floor on my way to the meeting. Plain and attractive, average and kind of cute.

Team leads from the other departments stroll inside the conference room at the same time as I do. I position myself on the second row near the center when the lights on the big screen display eight squares with names in the center.

One by one, each employee's face appears inside a cell on the monitor. I read their names and titles below for a more personable interaction when the time comes, preparing myself to pass whatever test upper management has curated with this meeting.

The face above the name Milena Reid takes me by surprise. Behind wide-framed glasses, she looks identical to the woman who ran out on me a few weeks ago. The woman I shared a sweltering night with. The woman who disappeared in the middle of the night and played me like a fiddle with a fake number.

I may have been drunk that night, but I vividly remember her soft, full features. Her fluffy, golden-brown skin melting in my hands. And her curves begging me to tour them.

I wait for her to look up, and when she does, she pretends she doesn't recognize me. She never loses her professionalism or seriousness for the duration of the meeting, whereas I've barely heard a thing that's been said from studying her name.

She told me her name was Natasha.

I stare at her until the screen goes black, then I leave the room in a rush. Back at my desk, I log onto the system and search for Milena Reid. There she is. Light-brown, mischievous eyes staring back at me through the screen. Round face holding up a pair of black cat-eye frames, and shoulder-length, straightened hair I recall pulling with my fist while she clung to the headboard.

Milena Reid, aka Natasha. A lying bitch.

Chapter 5

MIMI

My conquests normally remain a mystery. I don't bring them around. I don't flaunt them. I keep them in the dark, where some things are best left. Like secrets. And I can keep one better than most. My mother learned that about me at an early age.

But as great as I am about my covert movements, I confide in Sage about what transpired in the meeting over lunch.

"Remember when you said if you didn't like Charleston, you wouldn't stay?"

"Yeah."

"Girl, I might be leaving before you."

"What? Why? We're moving in a few days." She drops her fork on her plate. "That explains the strange look on your face since the meeting this morning. What's upper management up to?"

"It's not work-related." I sigh. "That young thing on the call this morning is what's up."

Sage's forehead wrinkles. "The little cutie pie off in the corner?"

"Mm-hmm. Remember the dick-and-dash I told you about when I came home a few weeks back?"

"Girl, stop lying. That's him?"

I look away while sipping on my sweet tea. "His name confirmed it. Jermaine Cooper."

Sage's eyes widen. "Oh shit. You did say it was Maine or Coop."

"Damn, I was fucked up that night." I chortle. "He was too. So he probably didn't make the connection."

"I don't know, Mimi. The way you described that night, I think he might."

"I hope not. I gave that man a whole-ass fake name, rode him to sleep, and dipped out like it was nothing." My fingers shake the table. "Who am I kidding? He doesn't remember me."

Sage grins, sipping from her cup. "Not unless karma has pulled your name."

I grunt. "They do say she is a bitch."

☙

The days fly by, and I leave Soda City behind. It's been a good home away from home—celebrating championships with twenty thousand strangers thanks to Dame Dawn, party hopping between college campuses, and being treated fairly on my first job postgraduation.

Sage and I move into our units on the same day, two buildings between us, with Sonya's help. Some friend of hers tags along and calls over his "available" buddies to tackle the heavy lifting.

I say to my sister, "I know what you're doing, and I'm not interested."

"Of course you aren't." She rolls her eyes. "But that's cool. I was just making sure you didn't have a reason to call ole boy since you're back home now."

"You know policing me doesn't guarantee I won't ever call him. If I want to, I will."

Sonya grunts. "And why would you go back down that road?"

"I'm just messing *witchu*." I push a heavy box against the wall with my foot. "That man is out of my system. Why'd you even bring him up?"

"Because you let one mistake you made in high school change who you are. You weren't closed off like this before him. You haven't had one serious relationship since his old ass did what he did to you, but I'm sure he's continued to live his life, guilt-free, and possibly find love. You deserve that too."

"Who says I haven't?"

Sonya stops ripping the tape from the box in her hands. "Have you?" She smiles.

"I've been loved on."

"But have you told anyone you love them?"

"Yeah."

"Who?" Sonya's voice heightens.

"I tell myself *I love you* every morning after I wash my face."

Sonya sucks her teeth. "You will forever be a problem."

After being beaten down by the heat and unloading boxes in every room, Sonya's friends leave. I open a sealed package marked *kitchen* and crank up the blender.

Sage, Sonya, and I unwind to cold margaritas in the living room, sharing stories about old lovers and mistakes made until the pitcher is empty.

Sage falls asleep on the sofa, while Sonya and I share my bed. The quiet and unfamiliarity keeps me awake with racing thoughts about moving back home. I had run away from the mess I left behind, only to return and find myself facing a possible dilemma as if trouble follows me.

The hours pass with a fresh lie on my tongue. I told Sonya that my ex, Leo, was not on my mind. That

I'd moved on. But the truth is, he still occupies a piece of me—has for years, but not as heavy as when we first broke up.

I'm not sure if he's imprinted on a tiny part of my brain because he was my first everything. The first man I gave myself to and loved: physically, mentally, and emotionally. My first real kiss. One boy pecked me in high school on a bet. But Leo kissed me for real, with tongue and emotion.

How he made me feel had yet to be duplicated, and how we ended things ruined me in regards to love. I no longer desire it. The anxiousness. The neediness. The yearning, pain, and hurt. I have forbidden myself to ever care for another man the way I cared for Leo James and to never trust the illustrious words they speak or believe the lies they package as a Trojan Horse.

A part of me does want to see him, though. To see how life is treating him. If he's still as handsome as I remember. If his cologne smells the same: rich and mildly sweet with the soft notes of bergamot that instantly arouse me. Is he happy with whomever he ended up with?

But my pride won't allow me to call him. And with our history being as toxic as it was, he is the last thing I need to add to my newfound problems sure to arise at work with Jermaine Cooper.

I toss and turn, thinking about how my clean getaway wasn't so clean after all, and decide that when I'm forced to face him, I will deny we ever met and hope he takes my word for it.

CHAPTER 6

COOP

The start of the week surprises me. Monday is smoother than I anticipated after having seen Natasha—I mean, Milena—on the call last week.

The office buzzes as I enter. Light noise travels amid ringing phones and conversations on every row I walk past, and by the end of the day, I've survived without being assigned the duty of training a transfer.

Tuesday, a new sun rises, and so does the change of the wind. A petite, mahogany lady stands in the aisle of my row, twirling her head full of curls with her fingers.

Okaaay. That's what I'm talking 'bout. I remember you from the call. Shit! That means...

I lower my head as I walk by her. "Morning."

"Good morning." Little Miss Petite smiles.

I take a quick glance inside the cubicle she's standing in front of from the side of my eye and walk fast to my office. Once I'm secure within my four walls, my mouth draws up, and I place my head against my hands.

It's her. Ms. Liar Liar.

My mind wrestles with how to act when the time

comes to face her. I'm torn between coming right out and clearing the air or following her lead and pretending we've never met. Except, I told her my real name, and she lied about hers.

A woman has never riled me up so bad before, and I don't like having my power and my cool tested. More than that, I'm pissed I have to deal with this situation at work.

There's enough space between our offices to keep me from hearing her voice but not enough space to erase the humility her presence brings me. A brief wistful smile owns my mouth until I pull myself together and decide what I'm going to do when our paths cross.

How she left me in the hotel was cool at first. I honestly appreciated her taking the initiative to make the morning after less awkward. But when I called the number she gave me to check up on her, I learned it was a fake.

She played me.

I swallowed my pride, thinking I'd never see this woman again, and added her moans to the list of ladies I've pleasured in bed. Unfortunately, life has decided to taunt me, bringing her not only to my place of work but a stone's throw away.

For the first half of the morning, I stay in my office, plagued with flashes of the night we slept together. Her soft lips tugging away at my skin, her big body bouncing up and down on me with more momentum and substance than the skinny girls I normally fuck. Her luscious breasts feeding me when I curled into her, thrusting upward as she rode me like a stallion.

I snap out of it and get back to entering more information on my report, but not for long when more flashes of that night burden me into a daze. How the cushion of her ass jiggled like plum jelly when I drilled her from the back. How she smiled, looking back at me when she came. How the sheets were wrinkled and crumpled in the middle of the bed when I woke up.

"Yo, you eating lunch in, or you wanna grab something?" Donald breaks my daydream.

I blow hard. "Let's get outta here."

I lead us out of the building, head down but on alert of the people I pass along the way. Stomping on the hot black pavement, Donald is on my heels.

"Yo! Slow up, Coop! Why are you racing?"

"I've been in my office all morning. I need this break."

"My workload's been light since my transfer got in. I can actually take a fifteen-minute break now. How is yours working out?"

I unlock the door. "Haven't met him or her yet."

⌘

The sizzling fajita I order would go great with a bottle of Corona, but the hour is early, and I have four more to get through with a clear head.

Donald sits back. "Have you checked out any of the fresh meat?"

"Nah."

His brow lifts. "They brought in a few head turners. I ain't got names yet, though."

"Careful. You already got one baby floating out here. Don't fuck around and get two and, on top of that, have to work with two baby mamas." I click my teeth. "Do your dirt somewhere else."

Donald poses with his fingers on his chin. "Oh, I see what's happening here. You're trying to block me out on the field and tackle the rookies by yourself."

"You sound ridiculous. My pops taught me not to eat where I shit."

"You ain't never hit nothing on the job?"

"Never." I cough. "Well, not on purpose."

Donald's hands flail. "I don't even know what the fuck that means, man."

I take a few sips of my soda. "Wish I could have something stronger than this right now."

"You feenin' a drink? This early in the day? Now I know something's up."

I bite into my dish, annoyed at Donald smacking on tacos dipped into his rice and beans. He catches me peering at him, and we burst into laughter.

"Look, man. I'm about to tell you something. And if you clown me, I'll never tell you another thing again."

"Cool." He continues to smack then wipes his mouth.

"I live by my old man's teachings. I swore to his advice to never hook up with chicks on the job. But damn. One of the transfers is a girl I smashed a few weeks back."

"So what? You that rigid that you can't work with the woman because y'all fucked?"

"No. It's 'cause we fucked, then she dipped out on me while I was sleeping and gave me a fake number and name."

Donald snickers. I stare at him like he's lost his mind until he calms down and bites more of his lunch.

"You said I couldn't clown you. You didn't say I couldn't laugh at your punk ass," he says with a mouthful. "Ole girl brought you down to size. Knocked you off that high horse, I see."

"Whatever, man."

"I'm for real. *We cool and all*, but you know you got a little chip on your shoulder. She humbled you. Good for her."

"Wow. I thought you were my boy."

"I *am* your boy, and that reason alone gives me the privilege to tell you to shake that shit off. She got hers. You got yours. She got you in your feelings. You got ghosted, per se." Donald chuckles. "Life goes on." He loads his mouth again. "I think you wanna hit it again. That's your real problem."

I raise my hand for the check. "Okay, wrap this shit up to go."

I tolerate Donald clowning me like he said he wouldn't on the way back to the office. I'd kick him out on the side of the road if I couldn't take a good, light-hearted roastin'.

By the time we make it back to the office, I'm in a better mood thanks to Donald spitting a joke I can't resist laughing at. It lifts my spirits, and we dap then split up once inside the building.

I catch the elevator to my floor. The coast is clear on my path toward my office. Relieved, I exhale deeply as I open my to-go box to finish my lunch in peace.

"Hi. I'm Sage." She startles me, standing in the doorway. "We met earlier, but I was wrapped up in the middle of a conversation and didn't get a chance to introduce myself." She extends her hand.

I close the lid on my food, wipe my hands on my pants, then shake hers. "Nice to meet you. Jermaine Cooper. Welcome aboard."

"Thanks. I was told if I had any questions to come see you as my team lead, so I just wanted to get acquainted. I'm a fast learner, and so far, everything I've learned this morning has been self-explanatory, but I'll reach out if necessary."

"Sure thing. Just give me a shout, and I'll help in any way I can."

"Thanks. See you 'round."

I sit back in my chair, listening to her tiny footsteps fade. I push my lunch farther away and unlock the screen on my computer, hoping my workload will make the last half of the day fly by like the speed of light.

Chapter 7

MIMI

Sage peeps into my office and signals for me to follow her. I ease into the aisle and meet her in the ladies' room.

We check each stall before she tells me what's up.

"I met him. He was nice. Polite. Professional. Fine."

"Of course he is. What'd he say?"

"Nothing, really. I did most of the talking. He basically said welcome and that I can come to him when necessary."

"So, can we assume he's not gonna be an asshole to work with?"

Sage shrugs. "*You* won't know that until *you* face him."

I fan her off and go back into hiding at my desk until it's time to knock off. The traffic of employees rushing to the exit is comically heavy, so I stay over a few minutes.

Sage steps in. "See you later for drinks?"

"Yeah. I have a few errands to run when I leave here. I'll hit you up when I'm dressed."

"Bet."

The sound of chatter and keys tapping has died

down. I log off, zip up my bag, and head for the elevator.

I step forward when the doors open. A body rushes into me.

"Sorry. You're supposed to let people off first. I should know this by now."

"It's cool. I shouldn't have rushed out like that." Jermaine steps aside and stares at me for so long I grow uncomfortable.

The doors begin to close, and I place my foot on the sill. "Well, have a good night."

I step inside and fumble with my bag until the doors shut to avoid eye contact with him. When it closes, my chest caves in, and I lean against the wall, happy with my performance.

Upon my exit of the building, the hairs on my neck prickle. I unlock my car and make a sudden flimsy move to look over my shoulder. There he is, watching me from the fifth-floor foyer near the elevators.

Proud of how smooth I handled our run-in, I add a little razzle dazzle while he's watching me and drop my keys on the ground so I can bend over. I spread my legs apart and give him a wide-eyed view to fuck with his head, then I laugh at myself skirting out of the lot.

Sage and I venture to a new lounge in Park Circle that one of our neighbors has been raving about. We pull up toward the end of happy hour and pass on the picked-over apps. A group leaving the scene provides an open table as the crowd begins to merge with nine-to-fivers and locals pouring in for the drink specials and amateur night contest.

I sign up to perform my brand of spoken word poetry. The metro has experienced what I bring to the scene, but it's the first time I have the courage to grace a stage in my hometown.

Two greyhounds later, the host calls my name. The juice eliminates any nerves I'd normally feel, and I'm lit enough to go up and talk my shit.

"You need any music, baby girl?" the deejay asks over the speaker.

"Something smooth and light will do. And Mr. Deejay, I don't go by baby girl. When I'm in your presence, I go by Queen."

Low moans rumble in the audience.

A girl sitting at the bar says aloud, "Aw, shit!"

Seated near a wooden boulder casting a shadow across her face, another woman shouts, "I know that's right!"

A male voice yells from a dark corner, "You talkin' all that jazz, you better know how to sing, big girl!"

"To the gentleman telling me what I better know how to do, I bet you don't know how to make a woman sing with your weak ass one, two stroke."

He quickly claps back. "I can show you better than I can tell you!"

The audience laughs at his comeback.

I return with my own jest. "I bet you want to, but baby, you barely got bass in your voice. I doubt if you're big enough to push in this cushion."

The audience woos and claps at my quip as a jazz instrumental begins to play in the background. I raise the microphone stand and wink at an old man sitting in the front row in a gray tam lusting me with his eyes. It breaks his gaze, and he smiles, then I begin.

CHAPTER 8

COOP

"*Well, have a good night.*" She looked me dead in my eyes, and that's all she had to say?

I stand at my desk, pissed I left my lunch. If I hadn't forgotten it, the weird brush-in with that liar pretending not to have a clue of who I am wouldn't have happened.

I throw the box in the trash can as the evening custodial worker pushes his cart to my door. I'm hungry but sickened now. And I have no taste for what's been played over and sitting out for hours.

That thick-thighed chocolate woman is getting the best of me. I speed out of the building and hop into my car with no direction in mind. Without thinking about it, I wind up at my father's house and let myself in.

I'm enjoying a beer when he makes it home, channel surfing in his living room like I'm entitled to do as I please.

"Boy, your car is blocking the garage."

"Don't worry about it, Pops. I'll pull your car in when I leave."

"That's not my point. What you doing here?"

"I honestly don't know. I got in my car when I got

off and found myself in your neck of the woods. You want me to leave?"

"Hush, boy. How you been?"

"Maintaining."

"That ain't an answer."

"I'm good."

My father joins me in the living room and cracks open a beer. He holds out his hand for the remote. I pass it to him, and his hand shuffles across the top of my head before he takes it.

"You keep a fresh cut, don't you, boy." He teases me.

The channel changes from the sports network to the news.

"What's *witchu* old folks and the news?"

"Gotta stay in the know. So what's goin' on witchu? Money? Your boss?"

"Nah, I'm straight."

"I know it's somethin'. Talk to your old man. Your dick ain't burnin', is it?"

"Jesus, Dad."

"Dad? When you call me that, it's somethin' serious. You done got some girl knocked up, ain't you? Didn't I tell you to always strap up?"

"I do. And no. I don't have a baby on the way. But..." I sigh and lower my head. "I hooked up with this girl a while back, and she started working on the job. I've always done my dirt outside of work like you taught me. Now I have to work with this girl, and it's driving me crazy."

"Is she difficult or something?"

"Worse."

"How so?"

"We finally bumped into each other today, and she had the nerve to act like we never met."

Pop covers his face with his hand. A low grunt sounds from his throat and grows into a loud laugh. I stare at him enjoying my dilemma for his amusement for far too long then grab my keys from the coffee table.

"Sit down, boy."

My nostrils flare. "It's not funny."

"You're right. It's not. I'm sorry."

"Then why do you still have that look on your face?"

Pop fails to hide his amusement. "Ain't no fun when the rabbit got the gun, is it?"

"Dad, I don't know what that means."

"It means the hot-shot player got played." He chuckles. "It happens." His lips curl, and his head shakes from side to side. "Dust yourself off, son."

"That's it?"

His eyes stretch at the television. "That's it. You can't un-ring a bell you've already rung. You go to work. Do your job. And leave it 'lone."

"Pop, she looked me in my face."

"What did you want her to do? Talk about that night that seems to matter more to you than it did to her?" His brow raises at me. "I know I said you can't un-ring a bell a second ago, but did you ring it at all?" His brows raise.

I stick out my chest. "I handled my business."

"Okay. Okay." He holds up his hands. "Then, am I right? Did that night mean somethin' to ya?"

"I'd rather not get into all the details, Pop."

"Pop? There's my boy. I get the feeling you like this girl. *What she* look like?"

"Not my usual type. Big breasts. Long hair—at least I think it's her hair. Almond eyes. Thick. Real thick. Big legs. Ass you can see from the front."

"So you can't throw this one around, huh?"

I blush. "I threw her around pretty good."

We share a laugh.

"But you do like her?"

"I could have. Now I think I hate her."

Pop chuckles under a smile. "That's just your bruised ego talkin'. Take my advice, son. She's got you goin' in circles. It's best to leave it 'lone. Do what she's doin'. Act like nothin' happened."

My phone rings.

"I hear you, Pop. I gotta take this. 'Sup, D?"

"Some of the newbies is hanging out here at the spot in the circle. Your girl and her new friend are looking mighty good. You coming through?"

"I'm hanging with my old man right now."

Pop shouts, "No, he's not! His old man is headed to a poker game!"

I swing by my house, shower, and change into something casual. Donald has a seat saved for me between him and his brother at a high table across from the bar. The waitress brings me a beer.

"I already had one of these with my old man, so I'm cutting myself off early tonight," I say.

Donald points to the stage. "You arrived just in time."

I look to the front of the room, and a man shouts, "Go 'head, big girl, *whatchu gon* do?"

I sit in my seat with the exact question in mind.

CHAPTER 9

MIMI

A man yells out at me, "Go 'head, big girl, *whatchu gon* do?" It's the second time I've been called a big girl tonight, so I scrap the new poem I planned to recite and pull one of my favorites from my arsenal.

I find my heckler in the dark and focus on the glare in his liquored eyes. My gaze locks his attention with a grin on the side of my mouth as adrenaline pumps through my veins, causing my heart to beat like I've just run a race, until a swift sense of calm showers me.

The chill instrumental playing in the background gratifies my mood. I'm in the zone. Ready to be my alter ego. And I exhale a deep breath and let Queen take over.

Aww, two guys called me Big Girl tonight.
Well, this big girl is a queen,
and that's what you will call me. Alright.

Don't get me wrong, size matters,
but that don't apply to real women.
Cause if that dick ain't thick and long,
You gets no access to swim in

Or poke around this big girl's trim and,
While I have your attention, may I add—fuck
your opinion
Got nerve to be passing judgment
when you walking around with a minion.

If you're fit,
Good for you, I respect your choice
So respect mine to be this luscious,
Juicy, fluffy, and moist.

The concern for my BMI is odd I'll say
Address me properly or be told to BMA

For those that don't know, that means bitch
move aside
Ya see I have a list of requirements and rules to
abide
You gotta be this tall and this wide to get on
this ride
And baby, when I say it's always ready to slip and
slide
This wet pussy'll make ya forget about your
motherfuckin' pride

One time I smothered my lover's face with all
this ass—
he almost died
Had him shivering and coming 'til that
motherfucker cried
And cream-pied until the Spotify playlist was
fried
Turns out he lied
Since the first time I let him inside
He likes fuckin' with big girls
A fact he can no longer hide.

Every woman in the house applauds me as I exit stage left. A few men refuse to clap, though smiles were on mostly all their faces. A few whistles blend in with the praises coming at me from every angle.

"That big girl showed you what she could do!" said a man's voice mixed in with the crowd.

As I walk back to the table, people tap my shoulder and pull on my arm to tell me they enjoyed my performance. Queen lives off of the stage for a little while longer, slowly disappearing as I return to my true self.

I take my seat.

"The gentleman in the corner sent this for you." A waitress sets a glass with an umbrella and skinny straw in front of me.

"What does he look like?" I ask her.

Her lips press together, and Sage and I laugh.

"If he asks, tell him I said thank you...I guess."

"I haven't seen you in here before, so I'll give you a heads up. He's persistent. Good luck."

As I sip the free drink, eyes stare at me from every direction. Thankfully, the attention dies down when the next performer takes the stage. A second drink arrives to the table.

"I told you," says the waitress.

I slide it in front of Sage. "Men hate when you give a drink they bought you to someone else."

The three of us laugh.

I say to Sage, "Let's get out of here when you finish that."

"Say less. There aren't any prospects in here anyway."

A man approaches her as she says those words. "You look like a good dancer. Feel like proving me right?"

Sage and I grin at each other.

"I don't think anyone has ever asked me to dance like that," she says to him.

He holds out his hand. "Come on. Show me before the song is over."

I watch the stranger and my friend laugh and smile as they bump into each other on the open floor. As they enjoy their dance, I slip my straw into the free drink and finish it off so we can leave when she's done gyrating on the guy smiling in her face.

"Do you and your friend share everything like you do drinks?"

I roll my eyes. "Let me guess. You're the kind man who sent these over?" I push the drinks to the center of the table.

He blinds me with a top row of gold teeth and diamonds. "Order what you want. I got you."

"Thank you, but we're leaving when my friend is done dancing."

"It's still early, baby."

"Again. Thank you, but no thanks." I grab our purses and shoot for the door.

The haggler begins to follow me.

"Don't do that. I don't need anyone telling my husband they saw me with a man."

He holds up his hands. "My bad, baby. My bad. You come find me when that don't work out."

I shake my head and blend into the crowd huddled near the exit. A hand strokes my lower back. I turn around with furrowed brows and a lashing ready to spew from my tongue.

"So, should I call you Queen, Milena, or Natasha tonight?"

CHAPTER 10

COOP

I stand before her with a sober mind, unlike the first time we met in a place like this. While I wait for her reply, I inhale her lavender-infused scent. It's way more pleasing than the smell of smoke traveling inside from the bouncer at the door.

The singer on stage ends her set, and Milena's lips part. I gaze deep into her eyes, waiting to hear her response, studying them for her tell when she lies to me.

"What are the odds two people would bump into each other twice in one day?" she says.

"Twice today. Three times this lifetime."

Her pupils dilate, and she scowls. "I'm sorry?"

There it is. Expanded eyes and a scowl of denial. She can pretend she doesn't know what I'm talking about, but those eyes of hers have abandoned her game.

"You haven't answered my question. What's your name?" My hand forces her body to lean into me.

"We met earlier today, but I was in a rush and didn't get your name. I'm Milena."

"Milena. Right. Is Natasha your middle name?"

"No. Why do you keep referencing that name to me?"

I scoff through a smile.

Okay. I'll play along.

"Nice seeing you again."

She studies me up close but says nothing. My gaze breaks, and I observe her in return. The crescent moon-shaped scar below her right eye. The tiny dip on the peak of her nose. The suppleness of her brownish pink-coated lips.

"If this is how you want things to be between us since we're now working together, I understand. I'll follow your lead."

"I have no idea what you're talking about. What's your name?" she asks.

Ooooooh she's good. Infuriatingly good.

"So, we're really doing this?" My fingers press deep into her back. She doesn't budge or try to remove them. I feel her squeezing her womanhood against my jeans. "Jermaine Cooper is the name. My friends call me Maine or Coop—the latter mostly."

"Well, like I said earlier, Jermaine. Have a good night. Nice to put a name with a face."

My grip tightens as I gaze into her eyes. She stares back into mine without blinking. I lick my lips then place my mouth close to hers. I smell the fruit and alcohol on her breath, inhale the aroma, then exhale the beer and mint from mine into hers.

She takes it in, still not blinking, still gyrating her muscles against my tamed wood.

"Goodnight, Queen," I say, finally loosening the hold I have on her, and watch her walk away with the girl, Sage, I met earlier in the day.

Donald quickly lays into me when I ease back over to him.

"I knew you weren't gonna let that go."

I raise my voice. "You called me and told me she was here."

"But I didn't make you come down here. I knew

you would, though." He pats my shoulder. "What happened?"

"She's still acting as if she *don't* know me."

"Maybe she's embarrassed. You might have been her first one-night stand. Shit, I take that back. She was bold as fuck talking all that shit up there."

"That person on the stage tonight is the person I hooked up with."

Donald chuckles. "No wonder you got it bad. If she's as sassy in the sheets as she was up there, I'd be whipped too."

❧

Snickering in the aisle, Milena and Sage speak to me when I walk past them.

"Good morning," they say like giggling twins.

"Mornin'."

My hate for Milena is momentarily stifled by the full bosom barely peeking between the buttons on her blouse. But the fact that the two of them have beat me into work returns my disdain for her and spreads a little toward Sage.

Guess I'm gonna have to come into work a little early now so these two don't make me look like a slacker.

I grab my coffee mug near my screen but stand stiller than a mime not wanting to bypass the cackling hens toward the break room. A tap behind me catches my attention.

"Knock, knock." Milena stands, smiling at me. "I made my special secret blend of coffee in the break room. I'll pour you a cup."

"Sure. I'll be in in a sec."

Is this girl out of her mind? Suffering from a condition or something? I can't keep up.

I walk in and find her grabbing cream from the fridge. At the sink, she meets me as I wash out my mug. Our hands touch the nozzle. I pull mine away and avoid eye contact.

"I order this brand from New Orleans and add a tiny little trick to it that makes it *my* special secret blend."

"And what might that be?"

"If I tell you, then it wouldn't be a secret." She pours from the pot. "Now close your eyes."

I stare at her like she's insane.

"Close 'em."

"You want me to trust you with a hot pot of coffee when you won't admit we slept together a month ago?"

"I beg your pardon. Slept together?"

"Come off it, Milena. Natasha. Queen. Whoever you are. Do you have a syndrome or something that causes you to forget things? Because if you do, I apologize, but that would make sense."

"Look, Mr. Cooper..."

"Jermaine. Maine. Coop."

"Mr. Cooper, I asked you to join me for a cup of coffee this morning to sort out what you were going on about last night. I wasn't expecting you to go off the rails."

"Me?!" I take a deep breath. "I am not the one who is acting like they have a split personality or short-term memory loss here. You are."

She chuckles. "Mr. Findlay suggested we work on the Craig Steele proposal together. I'll go tell him you and Sage are already working together on that since you have an issue with me."

"No. No. Don't even try it. *You* have an issue with *me.*"

"Actually, I don't."

"Then, how long are you going to keep lying?"

She pulls out a spoon and scoops sugar into my mug followed by pouring drops of heavy whipped cream to the brew. She reaches into her bag on the counter and adds a Hershey Kiss to the blend, opens a vanilla bean biscotti, and stirs for twenty seconds.

She removes the cookie from my cup and bites it. "Mm-hmm. Perfect every time," she says then dips the cookie back into my mug. "It's best to drink it while it's hot."

"Will you at least tell me what I did wrong?"

She grabs her bag and leaves me standing at the counter. "You should be honest with yourself," she says, walking away. Then she turns around and adds, "Has anyone ever told you that you talk in your sleep?"

CHAPTER 11

MIMI

The food scene has more than tripled over the years throughout the city and surrounding areas. Hip cafes, multicultural tea shops, and world-famous chefs have set up bistros, adding to the Gullah cuisine home is famous for. But trying them will have to wait when Sonya invites Sage and me to the barbecue spot in Mt. Pleasant we dubbed as "the real deal" back in high school.

"Traffic ain't been like dis back ina day less a hurricane been comin'," I say.

Sage looks at me like I'm a stranger. "Say that again."

I laugh out loud. "My bad. I told you the way I really talk would come out more once we moved down here."

She snickers. "I'm just picking at you. I understood you with no problem. I get a kick out of you when you code switch."

"I get a kick out of my damn self." I shake my head laughing. "I see why they had those *please leave* shirts made during the eclipse. It's extremely crowded here now."

"You would think this is the state capital."

Sonya already has onion rings and three bowls of sauce on the table when we arrive.

"I don't play that double dipping, so everybody gets their own," she says.

"I was wondering when we were gonna see you again." Sage hugs Sonya. "Will those guys who helped us move be joining us?"

"It's just us girls tonight, but I can call them if you want me to."

I stop her. "Please don't. I told you I wasn't interested."

Sage sucks her teeth. "Well, I am. So far I've met one guy at the lounge, and he was cool until he asked if I was coming home with him after one dance."

Sonya grunts. "Seems on brand with the material we have to work with nowadays."

"And that's why I don't want to be in a relationship." I snap my fingers. "It's all gaslighting, games, lies, and lames."

"Working on a new poem?"

"Always."

Sage bounces in her chair. "You should have seen her at the lounge last night."

"I was knee deep in grading papers. That's why I wanted to have drinks tonight. To make up for blowing y'all off."

"Besides Nikki Giovhorny over here, you didn't miss much." Sage's hands flail.

"I live here. You ain't telling me something I don't already know. Everybody's been with everybody or comes with baggage, nonsense, and drama. I guess it's why I'm so interested in playing match maker. I've given up finding Mr. Right for myself."

I wink at my sister. "Are you ready to come to the dark side?"

"No. You'll tire of it soon enough."

Sage's lips smack as she chimes in. "I don't know

why Milena keeps frontin' like she doesn't have a heart. She's sweet on our..."

I shake my head side to side. Sage hushes and looks over at Sonya, looking at me with enlarged eyes, and I brace myself for the inquisition that will never end.

"Sweet on who?"

I answer for Sage. "Nobody."

"Sage, tell me, have you met this 'nobody'?"

I glare at Sage. She zips her lips closed with her finger. Sonya's eyes shift between the two of us until I speak for myself.

"Get that look out of your eyes. I'm not sweet on anyone."

"Mm-hmm." Sonya stares at Sage's nervous face. "Who is he?"

Sage evades her intimidating gaze. The waiter returns to take our order and replaces the sauce bowls with fresh ones. The interruption allows us a break in our conversation, and the lip smacking and slurping of sauce-dipped onion rings gives me a moment's peace from Sonya's inquisition.

Sage ends the silence. "I've only had crunchy onion rings before. These fat, doughy ones might be my favorite."

Sonya continues to probe. "You know I've only seen her with one man before."

I mumble, "Not this again."

"He came between us for a short while."

Sage scowls. "Seriously?"

Sonya nods then asks me, "Why haven't you told her about him?"

Sage adds, "Mimi has been secretive since we've been friends. I, too, have only seen her with one guy, and that's only because we ran into each other while on a date."

Sonya holds her phone in my face. "Give Neil a chance. Look how cute he is."

"Who is that next to him?" I ask.

"His no-good-ass brother."

"I'd rather go out with him. Hook that up."

Sonya sucks her teeth and drops her phone back in her purse. "Sage, you were saying?"

The waiter sets our drinks in front of us. Sage inhales and holds her breath, intimidated by Sonya's demanding tone. She looks at me with bugged-out eyes asking for my help. Like a puppy asking for scraps from the table, I give in and save her from my relentless, nosey, big sister.

"Sage is confused about a situation I'm in at work."

"Why is that?"

"Because I told a lie. And you know how it goes. One lie leads to another lie, and then you're caught up in a web of them."

"Well, why are you lying?"

I shrug. "Umm. Felt right at the time."

Sonya shakes her head then looks at Sage while pointing at me. "My sister doesn't tell me much about her dating life. Everything she shares is vague. I'm lucky to get this much detail out of her. Ya see, *she been* holdin' a grudge against me since she *been* in high school. I'm surprised she ain't told you."

"*I'ne* holdin' a grudge. I just know *you* can't hold water like you can't hold yo' *licka*."

Sonya's voice grows louder. "I can hold my *licka*. And I can keep a secret. I just couldn't keep *that one*." She cuts her eyes at me. "What kind of big sister would I be if I didn't snitch that one time?"

"Snitch about what?"

The table goes quiet. Sonya and I both sip from our glasses, waiting to see who will fold. Me, waiting to see if she's still a snitch. Her, waiting for me to rehash the details of the biggest fight in our sister-ship.

"The way Mimi praises you, I never thought you

two fought. It's obvious you both love each other. And it's obvious that I wanna know what you two are talking about since I am the newly adopted third sister in this trio." Sage blinks incessantly.

I laugh at her honesty and crooked lashes. "She's talking about the one time I had my heart broken."

"May I?" Sonya interjects.

"Go 'head."

"And note that I asked your permission, so it's not snitching." She takes a deep breath. "My sweet, innocent, little sister here"—she clutches my hand in the middle of the table—" was groomed. And I put a stop to it."

I slide my hand away.

"Is this true?"

"In her version it is."

"Mimi, in her senior year of high school, was in a secret relationship with a man eight years her senior. That is grooming—if not statutory."

"I turned eighteen one month after I started seeing Leo, so I was legal. And I was eighteen when we first got physical, so..."

"And we fall out because she constantly defends him." Sonya shakes her head. "Eighteen or not, that age gap makes it grooming, and he knew she was vulnerable and too young to be wrapped up with the likes of him."

"Leo. His name is Leo. It's okay to say his name, Sonya."

"I refuse to speak life into that devil."

Sage clenches her teeth.

I chuckle. "He was good to me. He never harmed me. And if Sonya hadn't interfered, we would have run our course. But she had our uncles jump him. And after that, he lost interest in me."

"Tell the truth for once, Mimi."

"That's my truth."

"That's your version of it."

Sage chimes in. "There's three sides to a story, so what's the third?"

"That asshole threatened to sic the police on our uncles, like he wasn't in the wrong, but when I pointed out that he would be sitting next to them in jail, he killed that noise. And Mimi still continued to see him and gave him the power to end things. I had to console my sister in the middle of the night, silently crying in her closet so Ma didn't hear her."

Sage pities me, leering at me with her head tilted to the side. "I'm curious. What did he say to you?"

"That he decided to marry his son's mother."

Sonya jumps in. "A son she knew nothing about, mind you."

"I gotta say, Mimi, he sounds like a real douche."

"He wasn't a douche to me, until he…" I take another sip. "Until I had one *final* roll in the hay with him on the morning of his wedding. He came to see me at State. Made me believe he kept his son a secret from me because he didn't know how to explain that part of his life to me and that he would marry *me* if the world didn't have a problem with us being together. He fucked me senseless all night into the early morning. Getting all of me he could, like a real goodbye." I take a deep breath. "When it was time for him to leave, I watched him walk away, waiting for him to look back at me, but he didn't. He left my dorm room and returned to his lie."

"You mean his life."

"No, I mean his lie. He never married that girl. And the child in question was ten years old. A baby he made with a girl when he was in high school."

"Why didn't you tell me this?" Sonya asks.

"What good would it have done for me to let you know I kept tabs on him?"

Her blank face agrees with me.

"In the end—the real end of us—I let him think I believed his lies. He'd pretend he needed to get away from his family for a weekend and would tell me I would always be his peace. I let him deposit money in my account for a while, fucked him a few more times because, my Lawd, it was good." I bite my lip and close my eyes. "But soon after, I phased him out when I found a bigger fish and grew tired of the games. And I haven't seen him since."

"But she's allowed her unfortunate experience with him to cut herself off from the world—I'll never forgive him for that."

"Sonya, if I agree to go out with what's-his-face's brother, will you let this go once and for all?"

"The brother! No!" Sonya taps on the table. "The brother is a no-good whore."

"Perfect. Right up my alley. Someone I can throw away."

Sonya sighs. "Un un un. Neil is the one for you, but if you ain't feeling it for him, give me one quality you like in a man."

"Easy. One with the kind of dick that makes me say, 'Hold up, hold up, hold up. Let me prepare myself for this shit.'"

Sage's laugh roars at the table while Sonya throws up her hands. I smirk at them, twirling a straw in my mouth when the waiter returns with a pound of beef and sides, right on time to shut up my sister's mouth.

CHAPTER 12

COOP

'*I fucking knew it!*' I rant and rave to myself all night. '*But what did I say in my sleep? No other girl has ever told me I talk in my sleep. So what if I did. Milena Reid is a pain in my ass that needs to fly away on the broom she floated in on.*'

The next day, I'm strategic at the office. I arrive thirty minutes early, work at my desk all morning, have Donald bring lunch to my office, and have him text me if she's in her office when I need to visit the pisser.

I'm successful in avoiding an unwanted encounter with Sister Jigsaw for the rest of the week, and it comforts me that she has to play her games all by herself. But my luck runs out when Donald returns to work Monday morning, preaching, "I'm done watching you wimp out, man. That girl *gotchu* hiding out in your office like a bitch."

"I'm not hiding. I'm avoiding. I wanna keep my job, but that will be hard to do when her shenanigans make me wanna put my hands around her neck. The less I'm around her, the better."

"You've gotta get a hold on this situation. Man up. Reverse the roles. Act like you don't remember her and see how *she* likes it."

"No can do." I suck my teeth. "We exchanged words last week."

"And?"

"And she admitted to...ya know...in her little annoying way."

"Then what's the problem?"

My hands run across my mouth. "I wish I knew. This chick... Man, she's driving me crazy."

"I can see that. Crazy in love if you ask me."

I stare at him, too stunned to speak. His face looks punchable to me for the first time in our friendship. He's lucky we're at work and I'm forced to refrain from laying him out.

"Well damn." Donald stands. "If I didn't know any better, I hit the nail on the head. You in love with this chick, man?"

"You sound like a fool. I can't stand that girl. Hate the night I laid eyes on her. She might be the reason I never drink another beer."

"Camping out in your office and now giving up alcohol because of a woman. You got it bad, Coop. I don't know whether to pimp-slap you or commit you."

"Whatever, man. Ey, you still looking out for me on Friday?"

"As far as I know."

"Cool."

"I'm about to grab some lunch in the cafeteria. You coming?"

I sigh. "Nah. You go 'head without me."

Donald shakes his head, muttering below his breath. "It's times like this I wish I was your big brother. I'd slap some sense in yo' ass."

"Say what now?"

He lies and changes his tune. "I said your Pops would not approve of this behavior."

I fan him off as Sage walks in.

"Do you have a moment?" she asks.

Donald's eyes roam over her ass as he walks away.

I swallow the grin fighting to curve my lips. "Sure. Have a seat."

"Did I do something wrong?"

"No. Why do you ask?"

"I say this with the utmost respect, but you've been playing keyboard warrior with your input on this project, so I assumed..."

"I apologize for that. I had to settle some matters and should've prioritized better. Whatever you need from me to make this proposal perfect, lay it on me."

"Well, I'm receiving pushback from the finance department. I was hoping you could use your seniority to make them run the final numbers we need to submit the report for approval."

"How long has it been since you requested information from them?"

"Last Tuesday."

I reach for the folder placed on her lap. "Say no more. I'll get what you need and look over what you've put together thus far."

"Thanks."

"No. Thank you. You've done your part. I'll take it from here. When everything is ready, I'll schedule a meeting. And you should lead the presentation since you've done all the leg work."

Sage presses her lips together tight before she responds. "It's nice to have a team lead that's fair."

"You say that as if you expected me to be something else."

She steps out of my office and waves goodbye with a sly smile on her mouth.

I meet D at the lounge after the happy hour crowd has freed up the place. Sitting at our table is his daughter's mother, Kayla from the licensing department, and Davida, her best friend and also my ex-girlfriend.

I say to Donald and Kayla, "You two make having a baby not seem so bad, being that you're both here on a weeknight."

"It's called having supportive parents who recognize you need a break." Kayla slurps the last of her cocktail.

I gently kiss Davida on the cheek. "How've you been?"

"You see me." She raises her brows and tosses her hair. "Killing it as always."

I agree with her, and immediately I'm reminded why we didn't work out. The girl doesn't have a single humble bone in her body—a very well-kept body. Tight and toned from six-hour days working in the gym.

She runs her hand across my stomach. "I haven't seen you in a while. Have you been keeping up with yourself?" Her hand drops lower, and her vampiric nails get caught between the buttons on my shirt right above my belt. "Let's go outside so I can see if my hard work has gone to waste."

I push her hand away and sit down. "Still wild I see."

"Don't act like you don't miss it."

The emcee walks onstage. "Y'all ready to get tonight's show started?"

"Yeah!" collectively sounds from around the room.

"Y'all are in for a treat. We've been wondering when this bad-ass beauty...I mean Queen...was gonna grace us with her presence again. She set the house on fire the last time she was here. Y'all welcome Queen to the stage."

I text D:

You coulda told me she was here.

D REPLIES:

I swear I ain't know.

Milena's eyes look dead into mine as she adjusts the microphone. I stare back into them, curious what she's gonna say up there. Wondering if she'll bomb this time around. Questioning which one of her many personalities she'll reveal tonight.

CHAPTER 13

MIMI

"You know, the last time I was here, I had something I wanted to perform, but someone in the audience got me in my feelings, and I went in another direction. Funny how that keeps happening, because tonight is no different. I'm beginning to wonder if the universe is telling me no one wants to hear that other poem. So if the shoe fits tonight, put that motherfucker on."

The ladies in the audience snap their fingers and holler in my favor. A heavy bass rumbles from the speaker as a slow hip-hop drum fades in and replaces the bass, and I close my eyes.

"I call this one, 'The Goods.'"
Do I want you or that magic you hold
Cause that thing is *swoll*
Quite close to gold

It caught me by surprise
Pointing at me between the eyes

Sturdy
Steady
Girthy

Ready

Then it maneuvered its way inside my prize
Had me willing to accept your bullshit and
your lies

I had to check myself
Queen, I know you ain't tripping over dick
Men give that shit away for free with the
quickness

Queen, so what if it's good, snap out of it
The conversation went something like that—I
ain't proud of it

But when I say I nearly lost myself
Good dick ain't for the weary
In fact, it's bad for your health

Mental, that is, as for physical I say claim it
You ain't came across a good one if you ain't
named it

I hear some stirrings amongst the ladies who
know what I'm talking about

The pied piper in my mentions, I call him
ShowTime
Cause Gawddammit I know I'mma get mine
Gon' get slow-whined, my walls climbed, and lips
shined
Choked, stroked, and yoked by that nine
Mmmmm
Damn I forgot my next line.

Y'all forgive me I gotta call to make

And a man to wake who's got some walls to scrape
Batter up

I sign off to the chatter-filled crowd and walk off the stage, laughing at myself. The emcee wraps his hand around mine holding onto the microphone, initiating a tug of war with me. I slide my hand from below his and give him the side eye.

"That man is gonna answer when you call talking shit like that," he says into the mic.

The audience laughs over the remaining applause and whistles.

"Shiiitttt. If he don't answer, something's wrong with him. Hell girl, here's my number just in case that sapsucker somewhere 'sleep."

I look back, laugh at the emcee, then shout, "Don't make me come back up there and start up on you!"

"Girl, if you were to start up on me, I wouldn't stop *you*!"

I fan him off and take a bow from the side of the stage.

"Give it up for Queen, everybody." He winks and smiles at me. "She's quickly becoming a legend up in here."

I make it back to my table where Sage has been babysitting our drinks. A woman at the table to our right gives me a thumbs up.

I mouth, "Thank you," and take my seat.

"That was a new one. When did you write it?"

"A few nights ago. How was it?"

"Nasty as always. Not as humorous as your other work, but you still delivered."

"I messed up on a line. Could you tell?"

"No. What tripped you up?"

I point to Jermaine Cooper sitting snug with some girl.

"She's pretty. You think he's had a girlfriend this whole time?"

"They look cozy to me." I suck my teeth. "And this is why I choose to keep it casual. Every man has one on the board and a spare in their pocket."

CHAPTER 14

COOP

I pass Milena and Sage coming out of the break room with two hours left in the day.

Sage stops me. "Hey, Jermaine. Did you have better luck with the finance department?"

Milena steps ahead and avoids looking in my direction.

"I was just about to email you. I dropped off the report when I got in this morning, and Morgan just handed me what we needed. Let's review the numbers tomorrow then schedule a meeting with Mr. Findlay."

"Sounds like a plan to me." She smiles. "Oh, and uh...sorry for not coming over to your table to speak last night. I didn't want to impose on your date and make things awkward outside of work."

"Date? I wasn't on a date."

"Oh. My bad. I assumed... Sorry."

"No need for that. It was just friends running into each other. That happens from time to time. Anywho, see you in the morning. Say ten o'clock?"

"Ten it is."

I zoom past Milena's office with my head faced straight but still manage to see her plum lips in my peripheral vision. Her feisty words from last night replay in my ear.

'Who was that poem about?' I wonder. *'Was Sage fishing information about Davida for herself? Does she know about me and her friend?'*

❦

During my meeting with Sage the next morning, I observe her close up. She's one hundred percent professional. Not interested in me at all, laser focused on the project, and her desire to rise in the company is clear.

We end on a high note and head our separate ways from the conference room. I spot Milena going into the break room, so I about-face and head to lunch early by myself.

Donald catches me in the restroom when I return. "What's good?"

"Nothing. I had meetings all morning and grabbed lunch a little early. 'Sup witchu?"

"I heard something and thought you might like to know."

"Gossip?"

He nods. "About ole girl. I heard she put in to transfer to the downtown office."

My eyes stretch. "You playin' wit' me?"

"Nope." His head tilts. "Thought you'd be happy to hear that news. If she gets it, she's out of your hair."

"I'm cool whether she stays or leaves. These past couple of days have been easy to manage, so, it is what it is—just took some getting used to."

"Damn. I would have been fucked up after that poem she performed."

I scowl at him. "You *were* fucked up."

"How so?"

I chastise him with a waving finger. "Not warning me that she and Davida were there."

"I didn't know Kayla was bringing her, and Sexual Chocolate caught me by surprise, too."

"How about Sage was *tryna* feel me out about Davida."

"For herself or ole girl?"

"Ole girl, I'm sure."

Donald chuckles below his breath. "I swear you and that girl need to work this shit out in the sheets." He sighs. "Maybe then you can tell her you love her." He runs off to his side of the building.

Early Thursday, I pick up my old man in the '65 Impala he passed down to me, that was passed down to him. We shoot the shit along the route to my job before he takes the car back to his shop to service.

"How you coming along, boy?"

"Pretty good."

"You seem like you're back to your old self, unlike the last time I *seen ya*. Everything work out with that girl?"

I shrug. "I guess. I've been keeping my distance and avoiding drama, so...yeah. It worked out."

'Don't tell him about that poem she recited. He'll find a way to use it against you.'

"You sure the car will be ready tomorrow?"

"Depending on what time the parts come in today. You got a way to pick it up?"

"Yeah. D promised to chauffeur me around for a day or two."

He tugs on the new gray hairs sprouting from his chin. "Cool. But I don't like you having to depend on someone to get around. I'll do my best to have the car ready by the end of the day. If not, I'll pick you up myself after work."

I hop out of the car, and he yells at me like he used to when he dropped me off at school.

"No clowning and do your work!" He laughs and spins off.

I shake my head and throw up my hand at him, then I look around to see if anyone witnessed his tom-foolery.

Inside, I bump into Milena in the break room—our first encounter all week. She's humming a tune as she makes her special blend, scenting the area with her aromatic witch brew that tastes like heaven.

My legs lock up on me while my words choke my throat to simply say, "Good morning."

Devilishly, she grins. "Want some?"

I have no idea how to answer her question.

"So, we're not speaking this morning? Okay." She returns to humming her song.

"I never know what to do or say when I'm around you," I manage to get out.

"I know you think I'm crazy."

"I wouldn't say that exactly. Peculiar maybe."

She pauses her movements for a few seconds.

"And I didn't say that to offend you. See. I don't know what to say to you. Can we start over?"

She turns around and stares at me. "Sure." She hands me her mug with the words *"Keep 'em guessing"* written on it. "Consider it an olive branch."

I sip. "You must have worked in a coffee shop or something."

"I did. In college."

"You should open your own."

"That would be nice. One day, I might."

An awkward lull finds its place between us. I break it before the silence kills our newfound cease-fire.

"Since we're starting over, can I take you out tonight? No labels attached. Just a fun dinner to try and get to know you better and listen to you tell me what I did wrong."

"You think that's wise? I wouldn't want your little girlfriend to get the wrong idea if you're spotted with the likes of me."

"What do you mean...the likes of you?"

"You know. A big girl. A thick'em. A real diva."

"Allow me to clarify. I don't have a girlfriend."

"You two looked cozy to me. And you did say you don't normally find women that look like me attractive."

I cough on the cup of joe. "When did I say that?"

"That night in your sleep."

"Milena, I was drunk."

"A drunk mind speaks the truth."

I sigh. "So that's what you have against me?"

She lowers her head then looks up at me. I wait for her to tell me no and that she's been torturing me for some other reason, but she says nothing. Her eyes say it all, staring deep into mine while her tongue holds her truth.

"Let me take you out and we settle this like adults."

Slowly, she lifts her round face. "When and where?"

CHAPTER 15

MIMI

Jermaine insists he pick me up for our date. I insist I drive myself. And just like that, we're on our way back to square one. At odds. Staring at each other. Tugging at the power strings to see which one of us will fold first.

"Planning an olive branch dinner shouldn't be difficult," he says. "Please, allow me to be a man, knock on your door like a gentleman, and drive you to the place of your choosing."

I cock my head to the side, trying to remember the name of the new restaurant downtown near Waterfront Park. "Fine. I'll make the reservation, and I'll tell you where we're going when you pick me up. Tomorrow night. Seven o'clock. I'm in Castlewood Villas. Apt 237." I walk away, pretty sure he's watching my ass. "And bring my mug with you," I say to him without looking back.

He arrives with a bouquet of pink roses wrapped in clear plastic, and I pretend it's cool.

"I wasn't expecting flowers. Thank you," I say, wondering which grocery store he bought them from.

"Your tone doesn't match your words, Milena. Tonight you're supposed to tell me what I did wrong back then, but right now I feel as if I'm a repeat offender, and I'm not sure why."

"The flowers are lovely, Jermaine. I appreciate the gesture. You're just supposed to take them out of the plastic before you give them to a girl."

"Seriously?"

I nod with a smile on my face. "Come in. I need to put these in water before we head out."

He steps in behind me. "Your place looks how I imagined."

"And how's that?"

"Put together. Coordinated. Similar to the way you dress."

"And how's that?"

He chortles at my habit of challenging him. "Stylish."

I grab my purse. "You know I'm just teasing you, right?"

"Like I said earlier, sometimes I don't know how to take you."

I ease up on him. "Good choice with the flowers." I spin the vase on the counter in my kitchen a few times. "They add just the right pop of color."

We both dance around the hard-hitting questions and settle for small talk in the car.

"Nice wheels. You plan on turning a profit on it."

"I would if it wasn't a patriarch heirloom. My great grandfather gave it to my dad, then he passed it down to me. *Whatchu* know 'bout cars?"

"Not much. But I know money. And I know classics that still have their original parts are worth a grip. And I'm not talking about cars so you'll think I'm cool. You've already been in my panties. You already find me sexy." I lower my tone and mumble, "You might as well admit it."

His throat swallows a big gulp of air.

"Relax. You've seen me perform. You know how I talk outside of work."

"I have and I do. I guess."

"Did you tell anyone we're going out tonight?"

"Donald. How about you?"

"No. I don't talk about my dating life with anyone."

"You and Sage seem close," he says, then his voice climbs. "Not even her?"

"Nope."

We split an order of stuffed hush puppies while we wait to be served our entrees. The flavor shuts us up, and the background noise of chatter, laughs, and forks tapping plates carry on until he speaks first.

"Milena."

"Call me Mimi."

"Only if you promise to stop calling me Jermaine and call me Coop."

I smirk. "Okay. Why the preference?"

"'Cause when people say Maine, it turns into a bunch of Terrance Howard jokes."

I laugh then stop myself and cover my mouth with my hand. "Coop it is, then."

"Thanks." He takes a deep breath. "So, how long have you been writing poetry?"

"Since elementary school. It came to me naturally. Do you like what you've heard?"

He pauses. "That depends."

"On?"

"Was that poem about me the other night?"

CHAPTER 16

COOP

The plaguing question rolls off my tongue. Mimi puts down her fork and leans her head to the side.

"Do you think it was about you?" she asks.

Her tone has me perplexed. I can't tell if she's offended that I'm prying into her personal business or flattered that I think she'd write about me. A smirk is planted on her lips, and I don't like it. It's her about-to-turn-up-the-heat-and-fuck-with-me face she's given me since she arrived, and I brace myself for the game of Jeopardy she's about to play with me.

"Your answer tells me it wasn't," I say.

"Who says my content has to be about anyone? I could be writing about a fantasy." Her arms flail, and she prims her lips. "Or how I imagine it would be to fuck my favorite celebrity. Or...playful thoughts that expose my darkest desires."

I'm at a loss for words.

"Do you like my poetry?"

"Yeah." I sigh. "My question seems to have sparked more questions, so forgive me for asking. I guess I was flattering myself. I better carefully choose my words so I don't screw up this date before it starts."

"We came here to clear the air, so let's do it. Why do you feel like you can't be yourself around me?"

"Have *you* met *you*?"

She looks at me with a whimsical smile. "I don't mean to make you uneasy. It's just my way. I'll try to scale it back."

I exhale a huge sigh of relief. "Why did you lie about everything?" I wait for her to answer. When she doesn't, I grin at her and continue. "The fake name... phony number. Then to add insult to injury, you pretended you didn't know me. Do you really need to ask *why* I am the way I am around you?"

"I get it. I've been a tad difficult."

I chuckle. "A tad?"

She snickers and gestures with her fingers. "Just a smidgen."

My shoulders finally relax, and I ask her, "Why is that?" I gaze into her eyes to catch that tell of hers.

Her smirkish smile clears. "I didn't think I would ever see you again when I gave you that number. I sure as shit wasn't planning on going to a hotel with a man flirting with me over drinks, but when I did, I was kind of ashamed of myself."

"So you tiptoed out on me?"

She nods. "Thought I'd save myself the embarrassment of you looking at me like a mistake after you said..."

I interject, "Even though I don't remember saying it, or know why I would say that to you, I want to apologize. I'm sorry. But I still blame the alcohol, even if you don't."

"Coop, I'm a big girl. I always have been, and I'm not ashamed. What you said just threw me off because if *I* wasn't what you were *used to*—your words, not mine—then why were you all over me at the bar? *And* if you were such a hot commodity, then why didn't you leave with someone who was your *preference*? Like the girl you were with at the lounge."

"Again. I'm sorry for whatever I said while I was drunk. Second, that girl is my ex, and I wasn't with her. That ship has sailed and sunk like the Titanic." I lift my brows until she acknowledges that she understands. "Now that that's all cleared up, can we press the reset button?"

A curve lifts on the corner of her mouth. "I don't see why not. I mean, after all, for a fella who says he's not interested in 'my type' you've been adamant in keeping this exchange going. Are you finally ready to admit you're besotted by my thickness?"

"Has anyone ever told you, you have a way with words?"

She giggles.

"And yes. I'm feeling you. Your body. Your essence. Your presence. And your extensive vocabulary." I watch her giggling cheeks relax on her face. "And that swinging round ass of yours ain't half bad either."

Her face is unreadable, like a master of poker. I sit in the lull and watch her nose twitch and lips gather on the side of her mouth. Our main course arrives, and the only words we speak are, "Thank you," to the waiter.

She digs in first then waits for me to have a mouthful of food to ask me a question.

"You've seen my place. When will I see yours?"

"Is tonight too soon?"

"Oh, Coop. I thought you'd never ask."

I laugh at her sarcasm. Ready to pack up my food and eat it for breakfast, and her eyes tell me she does too.

CHAPTER 17

MIMI

'I bet that heffa at the lounge helped him decorate this place. It's sleek and modern and smells of lemon furniture polish—like a house that's been cleaned from head to toe on a Saturday morning while your mother blasts Teena Marie and Rick James so loud it entertains every house on the block. Did he clean this place before he picked me up?'

As I look around, I pick up that Cooper might be a neat freak. He hangs his keys on a black metal rod on the side of the refrigerator and catches my attention with hospitality.

"Care for a drink? Water? Juice? Coffee?" he offers.

I leave the breakfast area and join him in the kitchen. "Coffee? As if you could make a cup better than me."

I spot a box of biscotti cookies on the counter near a clear jar of sugar, a plastic bag of confectioner's sugar, vanilla, and a pack of chocolate miniatures covering an at-home barista cookbook.

Cooper doesn't see me snickering internally as he reaches for two coffee mugs from the cabinet.

"Someone's been *tryna* figure out my secret."

"And unsuccessfully. Come on, girl. Tell me your secret. It'll be safe with me."

"You haven't earned that privilege yet."

"Tell me how to."

My hand rests on my hip. "Where's the fun in that?"

He sucks his teeth. "You and your mind games. Just come out and say something straight forward for once."

I hold my head up high and gaze into his eyes.

"What will that get me?"

"Say something and find out."

I place my hand on the handle of the refrigerator. "May I use your kitchen?"

He exhales through a grin. "Be my guest."

A carton of heavy whipping cream stares at me when I open it next to a store brand flavored creamer and a container of whole milk. I chortle then place the milk and heavy cream on the counter.

As I reach for a bowl in the dishwasher, above it I notice a brand-new hand mixer sitting on top of the box it came in. I get tickled that I've had an influence on him. More than that scrawny thing he was sitting next to at the club, who wouldn't know how to bake premade cookie dough.

'He bought a blender because of me.'

He watches me open drawers for silverware and pull out a pan from the lower cupboard.

"Is there a special step to brew the coffee in the machine?" he asks.

"Not for what I'm making you. But make it a double shot." I pour the milk inside the pan to steam.

His brows rise.

I tell him, "Blend double the espresso."

"Is it true you put in for a transfer to the downtown office?"

I shake my head. "HR really is a joke. How do you know that?"

"Is it true?"

"Sorta. I inquired about a position down there. I haven't officially applied." I breathe out a heavy sigh. "Damn."

Cooper's eyes expand. "Was I wrong to ask?"

"It's not that. I just realized if you know about my inquiry, then so does Mr. Findlay. Reason 51 why corporate offices suck. Everybody is in your business." I pour the cream and powdered sugar in the bowl, blend it with a spoon, then add vanilla. "Got any cinnamon? Good spices? Or cocoa powder?"

"The only powder I have is the one you just used."

I plug in the mixer.

"And this." He holds up a bag of espresso powder.

I smile at him. "You really have been trying, haven't you?" I pause. "Should I not put in for that job?"

He takes too long to answer, so I begin blending the cream on low, gradually adding the powder as I increase the speed to stiffen the mixture.

The coffee maker beeps. I pour the blend into the mugs.

"This is normally served in tiny mugs for a shot."

"I have no idea what's going on or what you're talking about right now."

"Then pay attention to this free lesson, barista." My eyes glare at the book. "You're in the presence of greatness." I look at him, and we laugh together. "I thought it would make things better for the both of us when I asked about that position." Gently, I pour some of the steamed milk over the brew while holding the foam back with a spoon. "Check out that design," I brag.

Coop leans on the counter. "I for damn sure wasn't about to make that with these hands."

"Now, let's give it a second. It should be strong from the double shot, but it's best to drink it hot." I clear my throat. "And you didn't answer my question."

"As for us, do you think going down there will make things better? 'Cause I don't see it that way."

"How do you see it?"

He looks into my eyes. "Like you're running away."

I meet his gaze. "Sip."

"What about that stuff?"

Coop points to the whipped cream turning airy in the bowl as we taste the cortado. He tells me it's good, but strong, and that he prefers the sweeter drink I made at the office while finishing the cup.

"I made this particular recipe on purpose," I say, stretching my arms wide.

His eyes fixate on my breasts. "Why?"

"You said you wanted me to say something straight forward earlier, didn't you?"

He nods.

"Well, a cortado gives you a burst of energy." I slide my finger across the bowl and taste the cream. "And you taking so long to recreate the night we had is offending me."

His eyes narrow. "I'm sorry—what?"

"Am I being too forward if I tell you I came here to be fucked?"

I swoop more cream from the bowl and insert my finger in his mouth.

CHAPTER 18

COOP

Her perfect tits push forward, and I feel my dick harden at the sight of her begging nipples pleading to be pinched. Before I take ownership of them, the taste of chocolate whip cream melts on my tongue. I close my lips and trap her finger with the suction of me swallowing. Her eyes call out to me, telling me to pull her in closer. To take the lead away from her and be the man she's secretly been craving these past few weeks. She needn't ask. I'm eager to be of service.

I yank on her thin, silky blouse and pop a button. Hungry to taste her lips, I rekindle the flame blazing between us.

Intentional, persistent strokes of my tongue intertwine with hers, breathing in her sighs of combined built-up anger, hidden desire, and sexual need.

Her blouse falls off her shoulders. Her finger leaves my mouth, and both of her hands run down my shirt. Mine caress the center of her breasts then unlatch her bra. I circle each nipple with my tongue, holding the left one captive as I nibble on it and fondle the right one with my fingertips.

Mild tugs on them make her moan. I test which

motion will make her come undone and graze her nipple softly with my teeth then suck on it firmly. She sighs. So, I pinch the other and follow with a circling motion to make it pebble. A moan resounds from her throat at the pressure, and I smile to myself, knowing how I shall proceed.

Gently, I peck my way back to her soft lips. Her hair wraps around my balled fist as I tug on it until she's looking up at me.

Like a tortured soul, she gazes at me with dilated eyes. I slow down my kisses while her miniskirt rises from her thighs past her hips. They're softer than cotton and as smooth as the satin that's about to be on my floor.

I feel for her panties. "You naughty bitch."

She bites her bottom lip. "Oops."

I slide one finger between her slit then lick my finger. "Tasty," I say then lift her fluffy ass on the counter.

I reach for the bowl. Two fingers gather cream and layer it on her folds. I tap what's left on each of her nipples then pull on them with a wet mouth. Her head falls back, and I drop to my knees, spread her legs, ready to please her.

The cream jiggles as her pussy jumps the closer I lean forward. I lick the cream with a wide tongue stroke.

"Mmm," she moans.

The sound is music to my ears. I lick more cream off of her abandoned pussy. She squirms. I press on her welcoming thighs and still her, face to face with her black and brown display of profound pleasure.

The chocolate flavor lingers after I clear her palate of the whip. Slowly, the taste of her big love saturates my tongue once I've consumed the cream. The familiar essence excites me.

I whisper, "A literal chocolate pussy."

I flick her hole with northern strokes until my mouth arrives at her clit. Her throbbing pussy doesn't fight when I prod two fingers inside and fuck her while my lips nibble on her soaked nub.

"I'll remember to keep you hungry," she whines.

I spank her folds then cover her mound with my mouth and inhale her world as a whole, holding it tightly until she gasps aloud, then step back.

"Put more cream on it." I nod to her hood as I pull my shirt over my head.

She takes orders well, widens her legs farther apart with her feet on the counter, and lathers herself with a thin layer. Mimi licks the last of the residue from her finger.

I give a second order. "Stick that finger in your pussy."

She circles her smothered lips and smears the whip around. I loosen my pants, and my dick bursts through the hole in my boxers, watching her play with herself while I groan at her pulsing playground throb and beg to be beaten.

Her finger enters her hole, and she cocks her head back. Her ass rocks back and forth on the counter.

I watch the show for a few seconds then surprise her with a clit kiss and add two more fingers in her slit.

"Yes!" Mimi shrieks.

"Let's see you come before you take this dick."

"Keep doing this, and I will."

I turn up the heat and pull back to witness her release. Three fingers fuck her pussy while a fourth rubs her into a locked shake.

She pulls on my arm. "Mmm. Ah. Yes." She sighs.

My dick grows harder than it's ever been watching the thin veil of white cover our fingers. I place all three in my mouth and suck them dry then hold her upward.

"You will look me in my eyes on the next one. I

want to see them once I've weakened you. And you better not blink, Queen."

Her eyes widen. "Calling me that brings out my wild side."

I silence her with a kiss. "I know you have a way with words, but tonight is about show and tell."

I lift her from the counter and tread toward my bedroom.

She rocks her slickness on my stomach. "I'm starting to remember more about that night," she says then sucks on my neck until I lay her down.

With uploading passion burning between us, Mimi kicks off her skirt. I slide out of my shorts and grab a rubber from the drawer.

Her hand stops me from rolling it down. "Let me look at it," she says, seducing me with a hedonistic gaze that causes my dick to spring forward toward her mouth.

Her lips part slightly, and I shiver. Her neck rolls as she examines me up close, and she hums. Her hands wrap around me like a Viking war horn. My heart beats damn near through my chest as I wait for her to blow it.

"Firm as wood, long as a boat. How much of you can I take down my throat?"

She teases me with playful licks on my tip. Her hands massage my shaft, and I inhale at the sensuality of her warm mouth coating my skin.

I glide on her tongue. She pushes forward and closes her mouth. One hand brushes my upper thigh. The other prevents my full shaft from entering the warmth as she breathes through her nose.

Mimi pulls back and exhales then sucks me senseless with both palms resting against my legs.

"That's it, Queen. You got it all inside."

I watch her swallow and spit me out, taking breaks

to stare at my exertion hole like she's looking into a kaleidoscope.

When she grows tired, her hands travel up my thighs and return to my base, gently embracing my pipe while meeting her pulling lips working me over.

"Don't get tired on me, baby." I grab the back of her head and feed my dick down her *oral* compass.

She takes my instruction, my rhythm, and my force with light grunts and open eyes. Snatching my soul with a wink that she can keep up.

I pull out and hold her chin. "Your Highness."

She smiles and lies back, lifting her legs in the air. "Show me you're worthy to be called a king."

I slide her to the edge of the bed and plow my wood inside her wet walls. Irresponsible and bare, we get caught up in the moment of full-blown ecstasy.

My calves begin to cramp from the intense pivots of my stroking her phat, tight pussy limiting my girth when I drive deep. The friction withdraws a silent cry from Milena and instills extra effort from me to break her.

Her shit-talking plays in the back of my mind while I slut her out and draw shrieks and moans from her closed mouth sucking on her finger like she misses my dick filling it.

I kiss the heels of her feet and nibble on her legs while drilling and digging and scraping her juicy, raw flesh.

The closer I arrive to our final destination, the harder I plow.

I spread her wide and lay into her. "Open your eyes."

She looks into mine. "I came a long time ago."

"I saw it. But *you got* one more in you."

I squeeze her ass and drive it upward as I drill down. Faster I thrust in her water world and hold deep in her river. She shivers.

"Don't blink. Focus on me." I hold her gaze. "I feel it coming, baby."

Her eyes hold still. Her breath hitches. Her face grimaces from the pressure.

"Good girl." I kiss her soiled lips. "Where do you want me?"

"On my ass."

I flip her big ass over like stacked pancakes and smack her cheeks. They wiggle as I reenter her gush and fuck her like she wants to be—pulling her back as she crawls on her knees across my bed.

I push her down on her stomach and press on the small of her back. Her ass sits in the air. Her knees bend out wide. Her toes en pointe.

I drive my dick around her landscape like a second-time tourist. I know where to go. The best spots to hit.

Sweat forms on my forehead at the pressure rising from what's to come. The hardest feat is before me. To, or not to, pull out.

Mimi looks back at me. She feels my dick swelling at the tip. She knows I'm about to explode. Her eyes dare me not to do as I was told.

I give in and blast my hot seed on the track of her ass, trapping my dick between her brown cheeks until my clip is empty. She rolls her ass as I spread the residue on it, then I fall beside her.

With shattered breaths, I exhale, "I know where you live, but can I have your real number?"

She inches closer to me.

"We've fucked twice now, so I don't see why I shouldn't have it."

Mimi rebuttals. "We had sex?"

I look at her, desperate to find amusement in her eyes.

She laughs. "You said something about show and tell?"

My forehead wrinkles. "You drive me crazy. You know that?"

The side of her lip curves. "The first three numbers are 681." She rolls over and brushes her head against my chest. "You'll get the last four once you've proven you're not a one-round clown."

I peck on her neck, and her snickering transcends into a moan.

Her request is met with ease, three times throughout the night.

Pride fills me with how I make her scream. The way her ass bounces when she rides me to get hers and bites on my shoulders when she creams puts a grin on my face until I fall asleep.

"4563," Mimi whispers in my ear to wake me.

I smile at the sound of her voice.

She pinches my arm. "What's that for?"

"Cause I earned that shit."

We laugh together, then my phone chimes from the other room.

"Your phone has been going off for five minutes now, Sleepy Head."

"I can't think of a soul that needs to talk to me this early on my day off. You're already here with me."

Mimi grazes my arm with her teeth. "Don't you go getting sweet on me, Mr. Cooper."

My phone beeps and vibrates with a message.

"Damn! Who the hell ain't sleep this time on the weekend?" I hop out of bed then return next to Mimi keeping my spot warm.

Her foot rubs against my leg. "Everything okay?"

"Yeah. My old man left something in my car. Says he's stopping by in a few."

"It's too soon for me to be meeting your parents. And definitely not like this... Do you have time to run me home before he gets here?"

I scowl. "I could, but I really don't want to. I

might suck at making coffee, but being a single man, I have mastered the best pancakes. I planned on making you breakfast and holding you hostage while we lie around on the couch in my t-shirts all day."

Her eyes say take me home, but her lips say what I want to hear. "If you insist. But I'll hide back here until he's gone."

Chapter 19

MIMI

Though we've slept together once, that night feels like a distant memory compared to last night, which felt too real and too right. The level of comfort I'm feeling around Coop surprises me —even scares me a little. I never get this close—and never this fast.

He whistles while the water runs in the bathroom sink. I imagine it's spick and span like the rest of his apartment.

I look around his room while he's occupied. The walls are mostly bare, minus a floating shelf with three books and a sand hourglass. The sheets are super soft and make me wonder a second time who helped him put this place together.

'Ex-girlfriend? His mom?'

He returns to my side of the bed with a soapy rag, spreads my legs open with his hand, cuffing my ankle, and positions himself below me like he's giving me an exam.

"Double chocolate," he mutters.

"I beg your pardon?"

"You'll get it soon enough."

He proceeds to cleanse me with care, as if he knows how delicate a woman's lifeline is after storming her capitol like an insurrection. I watch his raised brow lower then rise again as he dabs my softer spots then wipes with the drier side of the towel. I've done things and had things done to me before, but being defiled then purified by my paramour is a new one.

"I'm enjoying this." I place my hand on his shoulder. "I really am, but is there a reason why I can't take a shower?"

"We will. Together. This is temporary until my old man leaves. Since you insist on hanging back here, thought I'd at least clean you up."

'Fuck being a neat freak, he's OCD. Or just kind. Thoughtful, perhaps?'

He pulls a pair of boxers and a t-shirt with my alma mater on it from a drawer. "Here you go." He hands me the shorts first.

"Whatchu know 'bout The Bulldogs?"

"I went to State. Class of '21."

I regret opening my mouth, foreseeing where the conversation is headed. Coop covers my head with the tee. The soap scent lingers on his hands as he pulls it down to my neck. I slide my arms in and catch him staring at me.

'Fuck. He's a baby. Lie to him. Lie to him.'

I'm frantic in my head.

Instead, I deflect. "I never took you for an HBCU man."

"I wanted to go *outta* state, but they offered me a free ride, so..."

A thud at the front door breaks up the conversation.

"Damn, my daddy must have been whippin' the curb," Coop jokes, hopping in a pair of shorts.

I take a long, deep breath when he closes the bedroom door behind him. Sitting on the edge of his bed, I convince myself to apply for the job on Monday morning. Distance is my answer to end the best love affair I've known. I'm nearly a decade older than him, work entanglements are a bad idea, and our *situationship* began with lies, an insult, and a drunken one-night stand.

'What have I gotten myself into?'

Deep voices travel through the walls. I tiptoe toward the door to eavesdrop when Coop and his father begin to whisper.

'Is he telling his dad about me? Will I have to do the walk of shame so soon? How do I break it to him that last night was casual?'

The front door closes. Coop calls for me as I rifle through his drawers, looking for a reason not to like him—something that will make me find him weird and unattractive.

I ease next to him standing in the kitchen. His contagious smile puts one on my face and masks that I'm questioning our connection.

He swings around and hugs me from behind. "How *many you* want?" he asks, spanking me with the spatula.

I shriek. "We still have our leftovers. You don't have to cook for me this morning."

"I tell you what. You make the call. Pancakes for breakfast or dinner?"

I hide my sigh from him. "Dinner."

The front door swings open.

"Oh shit!" I screech.

Coop raises the spatula in his hand like a weapon. "Dad, what the hell, man? I thought you locked it on your way out."

"Apparently, I didn't. What's with you not answering your phone this morning, boy."

"It's in the bedroom. Dad, this is Mimi. Mimi, meet my father."

I swallow big. Not of embarrassment that I'm

standing in the kitchen in Coop's boxer shorts and a t-shirt with no bra. And not because his father knows that I slept over and rode his son all night. I swallow big and choke on my words, because Leo is looking at me the morning after the son he left me for has his hands wrapped around my waist—and is introducing me to him—but we're not strangers.

"Hi," I manage to mumble and wave to him.

"Hey." He glares at me. "Pardon me for the intrusion. Coop, I left you a message on your phone. Listen to it and get back to me when *ya* free, boy." Leo locks the door this time and slams it shut.

Coop pinches my stomach. "I don't know what's going on with him this morning. He's not always an ass."

"Everyone's allowed to have a bad day." I reach for my chest while my mind battles who to call to pick me up, Sonya or Sage.

"You're right. He's a tough old man. I'll check on him later. So what have you decided?"

"I have a taste for my leftovers. I also didn't know how to tell you, but I kind of have plans with the girls this afternoon. Do you mind taking me home after we eat?"

Coop's demeanor sours, and his upbeat mood shifts. "Yeah. Okay."

"Sorry I didn't mention it sooner."

"You wanna pick up where we left off tonight when you're done?"

I shy away from the eye contact he's forcing upon me. "Sure, if we're not all drunk and passed out on the couch."

He grimaces. "What if I take you to brunch tomorrow instead?"

"Either one works. Let's play it by ear."

CHAPTER 20

MIMI

"This can't be life," I say to Sonya and Sage.

I inhale the sulfur-scented breeze blowing in from the ocean, and close my eyes. I get lost in the warm air enveloping around us until Sonya hits my hand.

"You had no idea he was Leo's son?"

"Not a clue." I exhale a deep breath. "They look nothing alike. Coop's dark, and Leo's brown. They have different last names. And Coop has a serene and patient spirit about him. Leo had a sly way about him... Though, they do have one thing in common." I raise my brows in a daze, staring at the salt and pepper shaker until Sage taps the table. "What are the odds they'd be related and both cross my path?"

Sonya scoffs. "Karma."

"Whose? Mine?"

"Leo's. He shouldn't have taken advantage of you while you were young, and you said he lied about marrying the mother to break up with you. I told you that man wasn't shit, and it serves him right. Wish I was there to see the look on his face." Sonya cackles so loud the neighboring table grins our way. "Forgive me. I'm overjoyed." She apologizes to the couple then leans toward me and whispers, "How did he look?"

"Stunned," I say. "Like he had seen a ghost, and like he shit himself."

"I wish he had."

"Sonya, it's been years. Let it go. Everything worked out fine."

"Even now you're defending him. But I'll let it go, since you've settled the score."

"What score? I'm doing the same thing he did to me—sleeping with someone eight years younger than me."

Sonya cuts me off. "You are both adults. Well over the age of eighteen. I mean, the age gap isn't ideal, but still, you're both grown, consenting adults."

"*Former* consenting adults. I have to end it."

Sage and Sonya look at each other.

"You don't seem like you want to." Sonya stares at me.

My mouth twists, and I bite my lip.

"Do you?" Sage asks.

"No," I admit. "But whatever I have going on with him has been complicated from the start. *So what,* he has strong abs that could hold a wine glass steady and a kickstand I can't stop thinking about." I fan myself. "I almost couldn't take the pressure when he was hitting it from the back—and by that I mean I thoroughly enjoyed him last night."

Sage's and Sonya's eyes blink at me in silence.

"I also enjoy not getting caught up in emotions and rules and heartache."

"And now you have," Sonya adds. "You thought playing it safe would fulfill what's missing...love." She smirks at me. "It's okay. Some things you can't control. And love is one of those things."

"I wouldn't go as far as calling this love. I mean, I like him. A lot. But...for the first time, I can't formulate the right words to say."

Sage snickers. "Sorry. It's not funny." She drags

out the word and crumples her face for a quick second then laughs again. "But it is kinda, ya know? *Whatchu gon'do?*"

"Well, I decided I was going to put in for that position at the downtown office and put some distance between us." I sigh. "But now, I wanna leave the state. Start over in a city where I don't know a soul, can date in peace, and not worry about who I'm going to run into."

"Noooo." Sonya holds my hand. "I like you being back home. Don't leave. Let me hook you up with Neil. Problem solved."

"I kinda wanna say yes so you'll stop asking me. But the answer is no."

Sonya grumbles. "Fine. I'll set you up with his whorish brother. Just my luck you'll hit it off with him against my wishes, but if it gets you to stay..." Her eyes narrow in on me. "I thought you'd be happy I caved."

A new text message from Coop lights my phone screen. I reach for it, but Sonya grabs it before I do.

"Why would he send you two chocolate candy bars as a message?" She passes me the phone back. "Open it. I gotta know what the hell that means."

Flashes of Coop positioned between my legs put a smile on my face. Sonya glares at me, then a grin crosses her lips so big that it damn near forms a semicircle.

"Never mind. Not my business."

I clap my hands. "You finally get it." I roll my eyes with the smile still curving my lips.

Sage buries her face from second-hand embarrassment. "Girl, what did y'all do last night?"

I point at her. "Did Sonya pass you the nosey baton?"

The three of us laugh.

Sage bobs her head at Sonya. "I think she loves him."

I don't answer.

She then turns to me. "But do you love him more than you loved his father is the real question?"

The cab drops us off in front of my apartment building. Parked in a vacant visitor's spot, the classic '65 Impala sits in the half empty lot, mirroring the night's moon and street lights off the fresh wax job glazed on the car.

"My head used to bump the ceiling in that car a decade ago." I nod to Coop sitting out in the open.

Sonya raises her head. "Say what?"

"Think I'll take a drive with him tonight and see if I've still got it."

In a drunken stupor, Sonya comes alive. "Drive with who exactly?"

I nod. "That's Coop in his dad's old car."

"I thought you said you were gonna end it."

"I will. After tonight." My chest burns and becomes tight. "He wasn't playing 'bout picking up where we left off once I made it home."

Sage mutters, "He doesn't seem to be playing 'bout you." Her eyes widen as she cocks her head to the side.

"Which is gonna make this harder once I ride him silly tonight."

I hop out. Coop sees me and steps out of the car, meeting me halfway in the vacant lot.

"Looks like everyone is out tonight," he says.

"Including you. Where are you coming from?"

"My house. What about you?"

"We had dinner then bar crawled down King. Moja brings out a crowd."

"You seem to be handling your *licka* well." He gives me an amused smile.

"Am I? I could use a seat... Across your lap sounds good. Take me for a drive." I wave to the girls and yell across the lot, "Go in without me!"

"*You'n go'* introduce me to *yo'* sister?"

"I will...whenever *we'en tear up*."

Once we're inside the classic, I unbutton my blouse and place Coop's hand inside my bra. His fingers work their way to my nipple. He grins when it pebbles in his hand.

"I thought we were gonna play our next hookup by ear?"

"I only agreed to that because you suddenly seemed uneasy earlier. That's really why I waited on you tonight. When you didn't respond to the double chocolate bars I sent you, I had to make sure everything was cool between us."

I unbutton the rest of my top and lower the straps of my bra. The wire pinches my stomach, so I shift it to the side and unhook the clasp. The cool air from the A.C. adds an extra sensual tinge to my nipples pointing forward and ready to be sucked.

I sigh and ask him, "Where do you see this going?"

He turns the car down an off road and pinches me. "I don't know. You've been calling the shots. Where do you want this to go?"

"I'm not fucking anyone else. Are you?"

"No."

I turn to face him with pure lust in my eyes. "Would you be cool if we kept this casual?"

He stops at the four-way sign. "If that's what you want, Milena."

I unzip my jeans. Coop proceeds down the road

while I fully undress. I rub my panties on his mouth. He bites them with his teeth and takes them from my hands. I loosen my belt and lower the seat back as far as it will go. My heels brush across the carpet on the roof and stretch past the head rest.

Coop drives the car with one hand and traces my folds with the other, dipping his fingers inside my pussy to taste my essence. The car stops in the middle of the road. He unfastens his seat belt and wets my pussy with an open-mouthed kiss, tonguing it like it's kissing him back.

My ass bounces up and down. My slit throbs in ache of needed pressure. His pressure. For my pleasure.

He slurps on my folds then spanks it with light taps. I gyrate from the teasing as he adjusts himself back in his seat with a glossy mouth and shiny stubble on his chin reflecting from the lights on the car stereo.

The drive continues with his finger fucking me sometimes slow, sometimes deep. Sometimes hard. Sometimes soft. Sometimes doubled with another. Sometimes with one jammed inside my pink while the other plays with my clit.

My juice gushes, and he licks his lips. I grunt loud enough for him to hear me over the trap beat grooving from the speakers. I look up and see I've creamed when he pulls out his finger, and I inhale when he rams it back in.

The car veers off the road. I sit up and look around. Coop is pulled in front of a sketchy, abandoned building with half painted letters on the window. He whips his dick out and pushes his seat all the way back. I lean up and suck him off hard for a quick session then mount him like a bike.

I balance with my hands on the roof. My nipples are sucked hard and rough. My ass is spread wide in his hands. My pussy rocks back and forth on his strong dick while he groans inaudibly under my spell.

"Whatchu say?" I whisper.

"I love how *you ridin'* this dick. Ridin' it like it's good to ya."

"It is good to me." I whine in a low tone. "How *long you* plan on keepin' this up?"

"For yo' good ass pussy, *ain't a* end date in sight, baby. Oohhhhh!" he hollers, squeezing my ass together to seal our bond.

I moan. "I couldn't stop myself, so I'll let you slide this time."

He lifts his head and gives me a passionate kiss. "You sure you wanna keep this casual?"

I rest my head on his shoulder. "I don't, but it's for the best."

"And why is that?"

"So neither of us gets hurt."

Chapter 21

MIMI

Sonya is drawn up like a baby below a blanket on the loveseat when I return. Sage sleeps across from her, stretched out on the sofa, clutching a pillow. Neither of them budge when I turn the top lock on the door.

I leave them be and hold onto the walls leading to my bedroom. I grab the throw at the foot of my bed and cover myself, sleeping off the night in my outside clothes.

"She's in here!" Sonya yells, waking me in the morning.

I lift my head. "What time is it?"

"Time to get up. Mama made me promise I'd get you to come to church with us. Get dressed."

Sage pops her head in. "Hit me up when you get back. If I don't answer, I'll catch up with you in the morning."

"Bet."

Sonya gets a head start over to Mama's house while I shower. I dress in my normal provocative attire but cover my curves with a sheer scarf around my neck that hangs far enough to cover my breasts and drape a thin cardigan around me to hide my bum as much as possible to avoid the dirty looks I'll probably still get from the elders.

I throw my comforter in the wash and arrive at Mama's just as she walks onto the porch, looking for me like she's missed her bus.

She hollers at me. "Two more minutes and I was giving up on you!"

"Grab your purse! I'll drive!"

Sonya plops in the backseat. Mama huffs as she climbs inside my car then smiles at me once she's settled.

"Sonya said you didn't give her any trouble about coming today. I'll have her get you to come to service from now on. Everything alright?"

"I think so."

"It's either yes or no."

"I could use some clarity on a matter, but I'm fine."

She responds like she doesn't believe me. "Mm-hmm. What'd y'all do last night?"

"Got drunk and slept it off at my place."

Mama sighs. "You two just keep on adding to my prayer list."

I zone out in church for most of the service. The only time I find myself paying attention is when the over-the-top choir director flaps his arms like he's conducting a concert at Juilliard. While they sing like angels, I tap my knee to the melody. I don't pray. I don't overthink. I just sit there smiling whenever my mother looks my way.

When it's said and done, I dash to the car after the benediction to text Coop before my mother is breathing down my neck and reintroducing me to people I've already met.

Last night was fun. See you at work tomorrow.

I change out of my Sunday's best and walk over to Sage's unit. She welcomes the tall, skinny guy from our move-in day inside her apartment. Sonya's friend, or should I say Neil's friend?

It occurs to me this is why she said what she said earlier about not answering, so I leave her to it and take a walk around the neighborhood instead.

Happy screams from a nearby park draw me in. Children laugh on the playground, while older kids talk trash on a basketball court. I listen to the joy in their voices as I walk past and find myself in front of a small pond with wooden benches.

I sit for a few minutes and stare into the green water, thinking of the best way to phase out my fling with Coop. But it never comes to me. It possibly could have if I had sat longer than five minutes, but I swear two eyes study me slightly above the water, sizing me up. So, I speed-walk back to my apartment with burned skin, no solution, and a new phobia of Charleston's gator problem.

In the morning, Sage and I grab our coffee in the break room.

"Thought I told you to hit me up after church?"

"I swung by but saw you had company." I raise my brows and grin. "How's that going?"

"It's nice. You know how it is when it's new."

"That I do."

"How was your midnight drive?"

"Memorable...indignant...dangerous...naughty..."

Sage stops me from reciting my acronym with a raised hand. "I get it." She shakes her head, and I laugh. "You are a damn fool." She laughs with me. "You change your mind?"

My shoulders fall. "I thought about him all night. I don't wanna be the bitch to ruin him for the next girl. Hell, I don't want him *to be with* the next girl.

This is so complicated. Thank God I have a busy morning. I could use the distraction."

"My morning's pretty hectic too. See you at lunch?"

"I'll drive."

Mid-morning, Coop slides into my cubicle. He's never towered me at my desk, and ideas run rampant as he smiles down at me, handing me a cinnamon roll from his meeting.

"I grabbed it before everyone breathed over the tray."

"Thank you." I take a bite. "It's soft and doughy."

"Innit though. That's how I like mine."

"Me too." I take a second bite.

"You going to the lounge tonight?"

"Un uh," I answer, wiping my mouth. "I don't want to become a regular. Ya know. Me and the girls might go somewhere else later on this week, though."

"I feel ya."

My office phone rings. The I.D. panel is blank. I reach for it as Coop taps on the panel.

"Catch up with you later," he whispers.

I nod at him before I answer the call.

"We need to meet," the voice says.

❧

I order a salmon Caesar salad and sweet tea at lunch, happy to listen to Sage compare the men here in the lowcountry to the guys she's dated in the metro.

Her cheeks are flushed. Her mouth constantly yaps. And she keeps me entertained while I wait for the man I'm least excited to see walk into the café.

"I gotta admit, the men are better looking down here in my opinion. There's chocolate everywhere. Milk chocolate. Dark chocolate. Pretty white teeth. And the accent you managed to bury sounds better coming from a man's voice. No offense. I feel like I'm with an island boy." She giggles. "At times, I don't know what the hell Rell is saying, but it sounds good."

I laugh with her. "So you're just agreeing to shit?"

"Pretty much." She cackles, then her eyes grow big mid-sentence.

I look over my shoulder.

"Hey. How you doin?" Leo's deep voice addresses Sage.

"Fine," she answers then scowls at me.

His finger brushes my shoulder. "You got a second?"

He pulls out my chair at the next table. His hand touches the small of my back as I sit.

Across from me, I look into his eyes. They're slightly older but still enticing when he gazes deep into mine. The barely hidden grin on his lips reminds me of our secret rendezvous nights in low-key dives, surrounded by clear people who wouldn't be able to I.D. us. People who were just as much strangers to us as we were to them.

I smell him and recognize his scent has changed. The notes don't agree with him in my opinion. It ages him like the old men that used to sit under the palm trees with my uncles drinking beer.

He's not the same shade of light brown he used to be. Working in the sun has layered an extra coat of melanin on him that works in his favor, but Coop's deeper complexion wins the battle.

The longer I look at him, I see a minor resemblance between them. They're both attractive men, but different. Where Leo is rugged, Coop is sophisticated and polished, the complete opposite to his father's blue-collar work and other street doings.

"I see you been doin' alrigh'."

I smile at the memory of hearing him talk. The last letter of random words are never pronounced. I used to love that about him. Especially when he called me babe because the y was nonexistent to him.

"Thank you. You shouldn't have expected anything else."

His grin rises. "Wish I could say it was good to see you again."

"Well, you called me. And here you are. So…"

"What fuckin' game you playin', Milena?" Leo scoffs. "And since *when 'you* star' goin' by Mimi?"

I hold up my hands. "One question at a time, Big Daddy."

His eyes flash at me. I assume he's shuffling the repressed memories of me calling him that when he would go deep in my nature.

He coughs. "Wha's ya end game here?"

I slide my finger across his thick brow. "You look worried."

His voice grumbles. "Answer me."

The bass in his voice trembles in my chest. His buried anger is festering below a raised vein in his neck, but I can't tell if he's hurt, or jealous, or suffering from a bruised ego.

'Was I supposed to come back home and chase him? Beg to pick up where we left off? Is he pissed that his son found happiness with me instead?'

The waiter places my order in front of the empty seat at the table where Sage is watching closely. Leo looks at him then back at me with seething eyes, as if he dares me to walk away before answering his questions.

"How could you fuck my son?"

"I didn't know he was your son until you barged in on us."

"You ain't do this to get at me?"

"Who the fuck *are you* supposed to be?"

His brows curve. "Milena, stop fuckin' wit' me."

"Fate put me and Coop together. Nobody was

thinkin' 'bout you. And honestly, I don't have to explain myself to you. I only agreed to meet because we *shared* a history, and I want to put this to bed."

Sage calls my name and points at the time on her phone.

"Look, I have to get back to work. Are we good?"

"I *wanchu* to stop seein' him."

"And if I don't?"

Leo huffs and scrunches his mouth. "You're not righ' for him."

"Why not?"

"You know why?"

I laugh. "Let me hear you say it."

"He's too young for you."

"The way I was too young *for you*?"

"And he's my son."

"So tell him about us."

Leo sits back and takes a pause. "It'd be easier if you jus' stop seein' him."

"Easier, huh. I guess that's how you've always thought of me...as easy. I was easy on you back then. Easy to let you walk all over me. Do whatever you wanted to me. And asked of me." I suck my teeth. "I hung on to your every word and let you talk your way back into my life when I was supposed to be starting over at State. And easily you walked away with that lie about getting married."

His eyes bug wide.

"Yeah." I smile. "I know you never married his mother. If you had, he would have your last name, and I would have made the connection." I purposely screech the chair when I get up. "Now, I'm easily telling you to fuck off. I'll do as I please, and it wasn't good seeing you again either."

Leo storms out of the restaurant.

I rejoin Sage. "I take it you heard everything?"

"Why didn't you tell me he was coming?"

"I wasn't sure he'd show up."

"He's a striking older gentleman. I see where Coop gets his looks."

"It's also where Coop gets his gift from below, if you catch my drift. And they both fuck like they might have the blood of Zeus running in their veins."

Sage chokes on her straw. "Come again?"

I raise a brow. "I'd like to."

Chapter 22

COOP

Milena pops into my office at 4:59. Her eyes are fucking me hard as she stands in the doorway, halfway in and halfway out. She looks over her shoulder then back at me.

Anxiously, I wait for her to say what's on her mind. But she doesn't. She eases inside my office once the voices on our aisle grow faint then closes the door behind her.

The silence between us is loud. My chest pumps blood ten thousand beats per minute as she hovers over me and lowers her breasts to my face. They brush my nose before she rubs her face against mine and drops to her knees.

I exhale into her hair then lift her chin. "We can't do this here."

"I know." She unzips my pants and frees my expounded bulge. "Who says we're doing anything?"

"The closed door with both of us on the other side."

She opens her mouth and blocks her windpipe with my dick. I shiver, holding my breath and swallowing my sighs and my words. Three head bobs and a quiet lick seconds after, she zips my pants and stands up. She raises her dress to her hips and lifts her leg to my desk then swipes the seat of her panties to the side.

Cream hangs on the outside of her pink lips. She shoves my face into her pussy. I taste her sweetness then she yanks my head away.

"Meet you at my place," she says, lowering her dress.

I give her a head start while I wait for my dick to soften. The cleaning lady's cart squeaks up the aisle, helping my manhood return to office appropriate. I tap my mouse so my screen lights up when she walks in.

"Sorry," she apologizes. "I thought everyone was gone down this row."

"I'm leaving now. You have a good night." I power down my computer, take my time to leave the building, then drive like a madman to Castlewood Villas.

Milena greets me at the door. Naked. She pulls me inside and slams the door behind her. I'm met with a kiss. It's slow and full of passion and draws me in to wrap my hands around her fluffy waist where I pinch her warm skin.

We stare into each other's soul before she snatches mine. Her hands reach for my penis, and I wonder why a hand job feels so good. Is it the softness of her hands and how they tug and press on me, connecting with my pressure points that excite me to rise to the challenge? It's like she can read my mind—both of them.

I break the gaze and close my eyes. "Milena."

"Shhh." She shuts me up with a kiss.

My pants fall past my ankles, and she continues with the job she started in my office. Blowing me like she's making a withdrawal to pay her rent. She is owning me, and I'm terrified.

She sucks me with no hands. No gags. And hard drags. I look down at her and lock my knees in place as

I float back to the wall and caress her silk pressed tresses. I groan as her strands slip through my fingers and take a mental snapshot of her full lips making love to my dick.

When she pulls back, I finally breathe. Milena bends over the couch and spreads her chocolate ass wide open. I step out of my pants and stride toward the sofa where I slide between her wanton, wet walls.

Her playground is plentiful to play with. I smack her ass until she hollers and squeeze her cheeks between the rippling tiger stripes that bounce when I stroke deep in that pussy palace of hers.

I roll her supple ass around my happy dick that refuses to pull out from the addictive pleasure her pink acres soak around me.

She doesn't complain that I've put my seed inside of her. She does the unthinkable. She turns around and smiles at me, licks her lips, then falls back to her knees. I shiver in her mouth. My chest nearly caves in from soft kisses wetting and sucking me dry. My toes press into the carpet, and I rise to tipped toes.

"I just wanted to make sure you got it all out," she says then leaves me standing there with my dick in my hand. She returns with a rag tucked between her legs and hands me a damp cloth. "You need my help?" she asks, grinning at me.

"I can handle this part."

She winks. "That's a lot to handle. Let me know if you're in need of my assistance."

She places a wool blanket on the couch and sits on it, covering her thighs from the sides. I zip up my pants and sit next to her. Her nipples remain on high beam, so I kiss them and brush my finger between her chest.

"Does today's treatment mean I'm worthy to be called your king?"

Mimi laughs. "You are, but in my queendom, the king comes second. I come first."

"I don't have a problem with that. So what did I do to deserve this royal treatment?"

"I need to tell you something—a few things, actually."

I kiss the back of her hand. "What's up?"

"I applied for the position downtown today." She glares at me with a side-eye.

"Okay." I nod. "I figured you would. And it's probably for the best after what happened in my office." I squeeze her leg. "I wasn't strong enough to stop you, and that can't happen at work. No matter how much I loved it." I lean in and kiss her. "And I fucking loved that shit. But that was risky, baby."

"I agree." She bites her lips. "So, it's a good thing we won't be in each other's workspace?"

"I wouldn't say a good thing, because I love seeing you around the office. I'd say it's a safe thing."

She looks away. "I'm glad you're not upset with me." She rests her head on my shoulder. "You goin' out tonight?"

"I'm going out to dinner with you if you feel up to it."

She lifts her head and smiles. "I do. Let me shower and get dressed."

CHAPTER 23

MIMI

I have never been tongue-tied. Secretive at times... maybe. But lacking words to express myself has never been a flaw of mine, yet I find it hard to be truthful with Coop.

I've had hours to blurt out, "I have a history with your father." But I say nothing. I watch him swirl his fork around pasta, taste test garlic steamed crabs from my plate, and buy myself more time with him before I lose him forever.

A few weeks pass by, and I interview for the job. The supervisor calls my office and offers the position to me later that afternoon. I tell Sage that I've accepted.

"I'm gonna miss having you close, but look on the bright side. We'll have more people to talk shit about at happy hour."

We laugh.

"And if you're still gonna cancel ya boy, being out of sight and out of mind will make the split better for the both of you."

"You know, it's funny. We've never said we were exclusive, yet we act like it. Maybe that's why telling him about my past is so hard."

"That. And the fact that you're in love but don't

want to admit it because you think that'll make you weak. But trust, Sonya and I have talked about you behind your back. We both see it. And if I'm being honest, I like you with him." Her eyes expound. "Not that I didn't love you before, but I like seeing you like this." Her hands wave over me. "Happy, is what I mean."

"I was always happy."

"Yeah, but not like this, and I know you know what I'm talking about."

I say nothing, but the growing smile on my face gives me away. "I do enjoy him. A lot."

"Girl, just admit you love him."

⁂

The good news about my transfer is short lived. My office line rings, and the dreaded voice of Leo stings my chest.

"I need to see you."

"You mean you want to see me. Not gonna happen. What do you want?"

"For you to stop draggin' yo' ass and tell my boy it's over between y'all."

"Or you could just get over yourself, let him live his life, leave me alone, and forget anything ever happened between us."

"He has a right to know."

"But it'll hurt him. And I don't wanna do that."

"You act like y'all in love or sumtin'."

I don't respond.

Leo scoffs. "Milena."

"What?"

"Did you hear what I said?"

"I did."

"And?"

"And what?"

He exhales into the phone. "Are you saying you love my son?"

"Yes. I love him."

Leo's voice turns stern. "Milena, stop playing with me."

I listen to him breathe harder into the phone.

"Has he said *he loves you*?"

"That's none of your business."

"I'm making it my business. If you don't put an end to this shit, I will."

⁂

Coop and I meet up with Donald, Kayla, Sage, and Rell at a comedy show later that night. My head is spinning so much from the conversation with Leo that I barely laugh at any of the jokes, while everyone else is keeled over, holding their stomachs. Coop notices I'm not myself.

"We'll grab a bite with y'all next time. We're gonna turn in early," he says to them after the show.

"Nice to meet you," I say to Kayla. "I've seen you around, but it was cool hanging out with you tonight."

"You too." She taps the arm of a man walking by. "Do you mind taking our picture?"

The man takes her camera and snaps the shot of us in front of the Performance Center. Kayla airdrops the photo to everyone while Coop, Donald, and Rell bump fists.

"You alright?" Sage asks me.

I nod. "It's been a long day."

She hugs me and whispers in my ear, "Hope this girl is cool. Tell you all about it in the morning."

Coop holds my hand and swings it as we walk to the car. They instantly turn clammy in the night's heat, but I don't let go, enjoying the intimacy between us.

"How'd you know I was ready to go?"

"That guy was funny as hell in there, and you barely laughed. I can tell something is eating away at you. What's up?"

"My interview went well, and they already offered me the position. I transfer first thing Monday morning."

"That soon?"

"Yup."

"Well, we agreed it was a good thing, so what's wrong?"

"My mind is racing a mile a minute, trying to figure out the best way to handle a problem that showed up a few weeks ago."

"I hope the problem isn't me."

"Why would you say that?"

"A few weeks ago? That's when *we* started going at it."

I smile with relief. "Nothing about you is a problem."

"That's good to know."

"You know what. Never mind me. You wanna text the others and join them for a bite before we call it a night?"

He opens my car door. "I wanna bite something, but I don't think they wanna see what I plan to put in my mouth."

❦

I stare at Coop for hours while he sleeps. Savoring the moment. Debating if I should rip off the Band-Aid while we're both vulnerable, or allow Leo to ruin what we share.

He'd paint me as the bad guy to protect their relationship. Leave out the necessary details like how he approached me. Lied to me. Led me on. And told me nothing about him having a son until he used him as an excuse to leave me.

We leave his apartment early enough for him to drop me off at my apartment to get ready for work. Later, I decline his request to meet him for lunch with the excuse that I need to tie up loose ends before I transfer. I also decline coming over to his place with the excuse I'm tired and in need of rest.

By the end of the week, I've avoided spending any private time with Coop. But on Sunday, I show up at his place unannounced and pounce on him to make up for the distance I've put between us.

Chapter 24

COOP

Spontaneous. That's the word that best describes Milena. Her showing up to my apartment to fuck my brains out is something I can get used to. She can pretend we're keeping this thing casual all she wants. I know she loves me. I overheard her saying she does the other morning in her office.

Her popping up like this can't convince me otherwise. It's the thing women do to catch another woman on the premises, make you out to be a liar, or find you in an uncompromising position. The thing that lets you know she cares. She wants you. She's staking her claim.

Milena rides me like I'm a bull with a look in her eyes that confuses me. Her parted lips and moans confirm I'm handling her properly. Yet, her eyes have a sadness in them today, no matter how deep or intense I try to stroke it out of her.

She trembles when she's close to her arrival, so I sit up and cuff both of her shoulders. Stuck like glue, I cement her on my pipe until she's weak and kiss her neck while her head rests on mine.

"You good?" I ask her.

She responds with a grunt.

"I missed you, girl."

She wraps her arms around me. Her heartbeat is fast and strong, pounding the way I pounded her. I squeeze her back with my fingers pressed deep into her damp skin.

"I take it you missed me too."

She hugs me tighter as I wait for a reply. But she remains silent, holding onto me so tight my softening wood can't slip out of her slickness.

"Baby, what's wrong?"

She lets go of me. Her thighs pull apart from mine, and she hides her face as she eases to the edge of the bed.

"I..." She sighs heavily. "Jermaine."

My head cocks to the side. "Jermaine?"

Knock. Knock.

"Who the fuck can that be?" I hop out of bed. "I promise I wanna hear whatchu were about to say. Be right back."

My old man stands at the door. I open it partially and talk to him through the crack.

"Whatchu doin' here?" I scowl as I ask him.

"What?"

"I'm busy."

"I can see that."

"Can you come back?"

He looks away from me. "Any other time I'd say yeah, but today, nah."

My head jolts back. "Give me a few seconds to get some clothes on before you come in."

"Boy, I cleaned yo' naked ass."

"Pop."

"Yeah, yeah. Go 'head."

I shout at him as I pad back to my bedroom. "I'm glad you didn't use your key!"

Milena is zipping up her dress when I enter. I know she feels me staring at her, but she avoids looking my way until she's slipped on her shoes.

"It's just my old man. You didn't have to get dressed."

Her eyes shift past me. "Yeah, I did."

As I throw on my shorts, she walks past me. I pull on her arm, but my fingers slide down to her fingers. They connect with hers for a quick second.

"Where are you going? We were in the middle of something."

She doesn't turn around. I press on her heels and follow her to the front area, breathing down her neck while the sweet smell of hair products and perfume flow up my nose.

There's a strange vibe coming from Milena. She says, "Hey," to my dad without looking at him. And in turn, his nostrils flare as he glares at her.

I raise my brows at him. "This isn't the way I wanted you two to meet, but here we are—a second time."

"Son, Milena called my shop and told me to drop by."

She stands between us, shaking.

"Why'd you do that?" I ask her.

Their eyes meet, and she says, "I can't live with your threat lording over my head. Do you want to tell him, or me?"

"Tell me what?"

My dad places his hands on his hips and stares at the floor.

"Of course it falls on me." Milena slices my dad with a sharp look. "Your father and I used to be an item. It's a long, old story I don't care to get into, but he's been pressuring me to break things off with you, which is why I've been acting the way I have lately."

I cut her off. "You two have been having conversations?"

"No. Your father reached out to me at work and

demanded that I stop seeing you. I told him I love you, but that wasn't good enough for him, so here we are."

The room falls silent after Milena's confession. I look between the both of them and don't know where to begin. The father who could have told me this news weeks ago, and the stranger-than-fiction vixen hell-bent on playing games.

"Jesus, Milena, how many lies can one person tell? You've been lying to me since the day we met... Natasha. Remember that lie?"

Her face darkens. "We are way past that, and if you're throwing that in my face, then we never really got that clean slate, did we?" Her eyes form water in the corners. "And for the record, I never lied to you. My middle name is Natasha. The only thing I'm guilty of is refusing to acknowledge I fell for a stranger the night we met. And I didn't withhold that information to hurt you. I did that to protect myself."

"From what?"

"From this," she says then storms out.

The door slams so hard my windows rattle in the kitchen and vibrate throughout my body. My eyes meet my father's. For a man with quick comebacks, he has nothing to offer. No words to comfort me. No explanation as to what has transpired.

We stand there in the silence, listening to Milena crank her car and the squealing of her tires peeling away from my apartment.

"You should have said something sooner."

"I didn't know how to, but I knew you should know."

"Well, I do now, so you can see yourself out."

"Son."

"Just go, man. Just go."

CHAPTER 25

MIMI

I begin my new position with bags under my eyes. The lack of downtime from meeting everyone and training with my new team lead makes the early hours fly by, but by the afternoon, I'm desperate for a cup of coffee to keep me awake. Desperate to hear Coop's voice, even though I tell myself a lie that I'm better off cutting all ties with him.

Close to quitting time, I pick up my phone, which hasn't rung all day. If secret cameras are in my office, it's caught me checking it a million times, hoping Coop sent a text, or the lines malfunctioned and somehow one missed call would be on the screen.

When I make it home, Sage comes over with a bottle of chardonnay.

"Sonya is on her way. Should we wait to pop this baby?"

I place the flutes on the bar. "She can catch up when she gets here."

Sage pops the cork. "First day *not so good*?"

"It was fine. Kind of boring."

Sage smiles as she pours. "Missing me already?"

"You know it." I yawn before I sip. "The vibe is very different down there, and I'm the fresh meat."

Sonya knocks before she enters. "Of course you two would start without me."

Sage pours her a glass to shut her up.

"Chill out. She just popped the cork."

"What's with the bags under your eyes?"

"I didn't get any sleep last night."

"Nervous about the *new job*?"

"Psst. Please. I can do that job with my eyes closed." I take a long pause. "Coop and I are finished."

Sage and Sonya stare at me with their mouths open.

"I would say it'll blow over, but your face says you're serious." Sonya sips from her flute. "Is saying 'welcome back to the single life' inappropriate right now?"

"That's the thing that bothers me. We never said we were exclusive." I down the last drop of wine in my glass then slide it over to Sage for a refill. "Fill it to the brim this time."

"They never said they were exclusive, but they were in love with each other," Sage adds. "Like we called it."

Sonya folds her arms. "What happened?"

"Leo happened. He was pressuring me to tell Coop about us. I refused. Then he threatened me, so I figured it was better if I told him, because only God knows how Leo would have revealed our history."

"So what did he say?"

"He accused me of being a liar."

"You think he would have responded differently if you told him sooner?"

"Nope. He was pretty condescending. I mean, the situation is pretty fucked up, so I don't blame him if he hates me."

Sage rubs my back. "He doesn't hate you."

"If you want, I can talk to him and tell him how

much of a douche his dad is. Maybe convince him it's a mistake to let the past come between you two."

"Sis, the only thing you can do is set me up with Neil's brother. You know the saying...quickest way to get over a man is to get under a new one."

Neither Sage nor Sonya cosigns with me.

"About that." Sonya clicks her tongue. "The brother declined."

I raise my brows. "I don't know what to say to that." I hide my face from them. "Actually, I do. That slice of humble pie had my name written on it."

"I warned you he was an asshole, and Neil was the one you needed to get with."

"If you're waiting for me to say you're right, mark your calendar. You were right."

Sonya gasps. "You *are* in love. Ain't no way you just told me I was right."

"I confessed to Sage, and now I'll confess to you. I was in love with Coop. And now I'll get over him. I'm built like that."

Sonya lifts her glass. "The Reid sisters are back on the stroll."

I hesitate to toast with her. "You gotta rephrase that. You sound like we're about to walk the strip on Spruill." I look at Sage. "It's like Two Notch."

Sage giggles. "I gathered."

Sonya chortles and tries again. "The Reid sisters are back to breaking hearts."

I clink my glass with hers. "Much better."

Day two on the new job, and an eerie feeling takes over me. Something tells me I won't be here long. I look around the office floor in search of where the chill encompassing me is coming from. No one is paying me any attention from what I can tell, but the feeling doesn't leave me. I charge the sudden notion to paranoia instead of facing the truth head on—I don't like this new job.

It's boring. The people are cliquish. And it's clear the trajectory to be promoted down the line will be challenging now that I've learned how many family members occupy the company—from the old office to the new.

Before I know it, the weekend is approaching fast, and Coop and I haven't shared one interaction. I type his name in the company directory and smile at his photo. His picture says everything about him that I've come to know as true. He's kind. Smart. Dedicated. Professional. And cute as a button.

At home, I stare at the picture of us taken at the comedy show. The familiar feeling of sadness creeps in. The bursting pain of despair shadows me, jabbing at my shoulders to jump inside my body and take me down. Sure enough, they begin to slump over, and I feel that awful emotion of heartache welcome it in. And I don't like it. It's the second time I've fallen victim to its wickedness, and both times at the hands of Leo James.

CHAPTER 26

MIMI

Sage and I park my car at my mother's house Saturday morning and carpool with her and Sonya to the farmer's market downtown at Marion Square. Mama controls the radio while Sonya takes the wheel. She stops on a station playing Cherelle and Alexander O'Neil's *"Saturday Love."*

I sing along at the irony of the words then stop mid-hook. "Damn. This song is literally describing the opposite of my last week. Their love starts on a Sunday. Mine ended on one." I catch Sonya and Sage glance at each other and shut my mouth.

"I *shoulda* known you were wrapped up in some man-ish little boy. You don't come 'round much when your nose is wide open."

I change the subject. "How do you feel about the park since they moved what's-his-face's statue?"

She shrugs. "Damn that man and whoever wanted to glorify him in the first place."

"Amen," Sonya mumbles.

Mama walks ahead of us when we arrive to the market. I watch her mingle and speak to the vendors like they're old friends and wonder if I'm fated to be like her when I'm older—single, heavily involved in the church, hell-bent on saving the souls of the youth, and somehow alone, but not lonely.

As she yaps with people I assume she knows from coming here often, I watch her in action, picking over fruits and chatting away with people of all shapes and colors.

Nothing about her is miserable. She's happy. Mean at times, but happy, nonetheless.

While in her element of discussing gardening and the right season for the apples she's rifling through, I think back and realize I've never seen her with a man outside of my father. And though she's been alone since we lost him, the only tears I've seen her shed were at his funeral.

"Sonya, has Mama had any boyfriends you know of?"

"Not really. A few of the men at church tried to holla at her, but she never entertained any of that mess."

"That doesn't mean she doesn't creep," Sonya adds. "Mimi had to get that secretive behavior from somewhere."

Sonya and I frown at her.

"I dare you to say that to my mama's face," I say, until I burst into laughter. "I'm just playin'." I shake my head. "But for real, don't do that."

Sonya turns curious. "Why do you ask?"

"I was just thinking, if I end up alone, I might be alright, judging by the way Mama doesn't seem to mind."

"*I've* made my peace with it."

I roll my eyes, point at Sonya, and say to Sage, "She'll be the first one of us to get married. Just watch."

A wild walking fella bumps into me. "*Dese skee-*

tas'll pull up on ya wit' all dat smell good on." He smiles at me. "I know *dey tayin' you up.*"

I look him dead in his eyes. "Tell me about it."

Sonya and Sage cover their mouths and chuckle. I hear them. I can only assume this fresh motherfucker hears them too.

"Baby girl, *is you* callin' me a skeeta?"

"I wouldn't dare." I hide my hands in my pocket." They've been tearin' me up since me and my husband got out here."

"Oh. My bad. You married. You have a good day *den.*"

"You too."

We wait for him to walk a few yards away.

Sage says, "I made out most of what he said. By *skeeta,* did he mean mosquito?"

"Yeah, his slick ass was talkin' 'bout mosquitos. Y'all know he felt me up when he bumped into me, right?"

"Why you ain't put him on blast?"

"And embarrass Mama?" I turn around. "Look at her. This is her special place, and I'm already the problem child."

"She would understand. Hell, she might go cuss him out."

I throw up my hands. "Don't mention it. Crisis averted. Problem de-escalated."

"Speaking of problems..." Sonya nudges Sage's arm. "I hear a man ain't one for you. Rell really likes you."

Sage's cheeks turn pinker than the peonies at the flower stand we cross. "I like him too. I didn't want to talk about it because of...you know."

I cover my chest with my dewy palm. "Because of me. You know me better than that. I'm happy you're happy."

"We hung out at the lounge with the old folks

Thursday night. The owner asked when you're coming back to bless the mic? Apparently, people have been talking about you and poppin' in to hear your spoken word."

"Shit, sounds like I need to be getting paid."

Sonya chimes in. "You want me to negotiate that for you? His club is making bank, I'm sure."

I moan. "I just might say yes."

Mama interrupts our conversation. "The jam lady just told me another hurricane formed, and this one is definitely headed our way."

CHAPTER 27

COOP

Pissed off would be an understatement of how I feel. Seven days have passed, and I still see red. Crimson red to be exact, but the anger flowing inside of me is incomparable to the humiliation and hurt that's been handed to me from not one, but two people I love. Loved.

Goofy-ass Donald and his mediocre jokes are the only things to put a smile on my face these days, and the smile doesn't last long. But I'm grateful for the brief relief of misery shrouding me.

It's hard not to think of Mimi. I miss her. And when I see Sage at work, my mind creates an image of Milena by her side, staring back at me like she's a ghost.

Sage has caught me staring off in the distance when we encounter each other. I feel like a weirdo—not being able to explain I'm staring at someone who isn't there. Then, I'm ashamed when her eyes pity me. But today is different. One week of simp behavior is a week too many to sulk after what's been done.

Sage's curious glare snaps me out of my daze.

"How you doin' today?" I say to her, attempting to cover up my gazing at imaginary figures.

"I'm good. And you?"

"I'm makin' it. Getting everything in order before the storm arrives."

"I sure was hoping it turned."

"You ain't by yourself." I sigh. "But what can you do?"

"Oh, I'm leaving. I've experienced tropical storms once it's on land, but never a direct hit as a hurricane. And I don't want to."

"*Where you* goin'? Back to Columbia?"

"I was, but Rell suggested we take our first trip together, so we're flying out to Vegas for a few days."

Her response hits me in the gut. "Oh. That's what's up. He seems like a cool dude." A forced smile masks my jealousy. "Well, y'all have a good time. I'll be riding out the storm with my ma."

"I'll be praying for y'all."

A category three storm with the potential of increasing in size and speed is headed in my direction, yet all I can think of is if Mimi is going to Vegas with Sage and a new boy toy.

A million questions flood my mind.

'Did she tell this new victim of hers her real name? Will she pretend she doesn't know him after the trip? Will she fuck with his mind the way she's fucked with mine?' And most importantly. *'Will she fuck him?'*

That last question plagues me.

My conversation with Sage replays in my head all day. Visions of Milena's smile, her strut, and images of random men servicing her, calling her queen, and making her holler clouds my head 'til it's quitting time.

Old Man lights across the screen of my phone while I drive home. I send him to voicemail as I have all week. He calls back to back, finally gets the message, and gives it a rest.

I'm jittery once I'm home. I crack open a beer and try to relax while catching up on a show I've neglected since being entangled. It doesn't hold my interest as my mind is still on *her*.

The phone rings again, and I ignore it. I assume it's my dad again, but my anxiety tells me to check it to be sure.

D texts:

'The lounge is packed tonight.
Everyone's out before the storm hits.
Come out. Have a drink. Ease your
mind.'

'Is she there?'

'It's so packed, she could be, but I
don't see her. Come thru.'

I change out of my work clothes and put on my club best—fresh sneaks, khakis, and a furlow, lying to myself that I don't want Milena to be at the club, while my foot is pressed to the metal, hoping she is.

"Fuck me," I mumble when I turn off the engine.

Dad taps on my window. "Don't be mad at Donald. I begged him to get you out here."

I crank the car.

"Turn it off!" His hand presses on the glass. "A fuckin' storm is comin', and anything can happen. Let's settle this shit *nih*."

I unlock the door. He walks around to the passenger side, climbs in, and stares at me while I keep my head straight. My fists are balled, ready to bloody his nose—make him *feel* pain like I *feel* pain.

"There's nothing you can say to make me change how I feel. You should have told me the morning you saw us together. You let me get in too deep, and now it's too late. You could have prevented all of this."

"Boy." He kisses his teeth. "You were in too deep

when you first told me about her. She didn't go by Mimi back then. Had you called her Milena, I would have known."

"That has nothing to do with the morning you saw us!"

"I'm *gon' tell you dis* one time. Don't raise your voice at me. Now turn the car off."

I rev the engine. "Boy."

Exasperated, I finally look at him. "Just say what you have to say."

For the first time, I think he sees me. He sits quietly and stares into my eyes without a response. His flared nose and burning eyes don't intimidate me like usual, and he recognizes he can't talk to me like a little boy at this moment. It's me and him, having a man-to-man conversation I don't think he's ready for, and so I call him out.

"Do you still love her? Did you ever love her? Or did you play her like you played my mother?"

His eyes expand.

"Yeah, I know all about how you promised to marry my mama and never did."

"I raised you! I did what I was supposed to do! You never went without! I was at every game! Every award ceremony! Every doctor appointment!"

"But you lied to her! And to me!" I beat my chest. "You think I enjoyed having you wake up at our house sometimes and see her all happy, then I'd be happy, thinking we're finally gonna be a family. Then, two, three days later, see her *tryna* hide her tears." I suck my teeth. "I can only imagine what you did to Milena."

Pops withholds his words behind tightly pressed lips.

"All week, I've been replaying what she said that day. "I can't live with your threat lording over my head, and of course it falls on me." What'd she mean by 'it all falls on her'?"

He stutters. "I...I have no idea. I don't know."

"She even told you that she loved me, and that wasn't good enough for you to leave us be."

"Son, you couldn't build nuttin' serious with dat girl built on secrets. Trust me. I know dat much."

"When I wanna be delusional, I think, yeah, I could have had something with her if I never knew. But I live in reality, where my daddy fucked the chick I was diggin'." I roll my shoulders. "You can get out now."

"What you wan' me to say?"

"It's too late to say anything. Things might be different between us if you would have spoken up when you had the chance."

His voice shakes. "I didn't know how to tell you. I knew you really liked whoever it was you were seein' the first time you told me about her. I just wish you would have said her name that day, and we wouldn't be sittin' in this car havin' this conversation with God's wrath headin' for us." He sighs and rubs his hands over his mouth. "I can't be at odds with my only son over somethin' that's not in my control and because you wanna pretend what y'all had was perfect. It was flawed from the beginning. You said so yourself."

"It *was* at first. But we turned it around."

"So, no matter what I say, this is all on me?"

"I ain't say that. Mimi is responsible too. But I ain't as mad at her as I am at you, 'cause I'm yo' son. And you didn't keep it real with me. At least she tried to pull away from me after she saw you were my father, but I kept pushing, not knowing she was moving funny because of a threat. Pop, you could have just *deaded* everything. But you let time pass. And now, I'm in my feelings, and *I'on* like this shit."

"I'm sorry. I hate *dat you* goin' through all of *dis*. But I love you. I may have handled this all wrong, but what's done is done. And it's for the better. You'll meet your person one day. It just wasn't her."

"And if it is her, then what?"

His eyes narrow in on me.

"I'mma ask you again. Are you still in love with her?"

Chapter 28

MIMI

Every holiday, the alumni from downtown Charleston high schools and rival academies from the islands, both bridges, and way past the north area, pile into whatever club is popular. Frenzy surrounding the storm has the parking lot of the Park Circle lounge packed like it's a holiday when Sonya and I pull up.

She lifts my hand before we exit the car. "What is this?" Her finger presses on my ring finger.

"Something I wear when I don't want to be bothered. When I lied to that guy at the farmer's market about having a husband, I figured I'd pull it back out."

Her brows rise. "And that keeps men from *tryna holla atchu*?"

The tone of my voice rises a level higher than normal. "Sometimes. Sometimes it makes you more desirable to fuckboys out to game women, fuck them, and send them back home to their husbands like a rode hard heaux." I roll my eyes. "Learned that the hard way."

Sonya chuckles. "The things that come out of your mouth."

Our eyes meet.

"Forget I said that." She laughs. "Let's go in."

I ask the bouncer, "Where's the owner? I heard he's been asking about me."

He points to a short man, smoking at the end of the bar, with a pencil above his ear.

I tap his shoulder. "We'll accept free drinks all night if I perform. But after this, let's talk money."

He slips me two one hundred dollar bills from a clip held in his pocket. "You get up there and do what you been doing, and I'll double that. Twice a month."

"Deal."

Sonya whispers in my ear, "Ask for VIP seating too. It's a madhouse in here tonight. Ain't nowhere to sit."

"I'm gonna also need a table of my own."

"You can have mine." He nods to the empty center table below the balcony of the second level. "I never get to sit in it anyway."

The bartender slams two shots of whiskey in front of us.

"Cheers." He finishes off his drink.

"Cheers." Sonya and I toast, take it to the head, and hold onto each other through the burn.

❧

We laugh at the dirty looks thrown at us while sitting in the owner's booth. Every glance is different. Curiosity from some. Jealousy from others. Intrigue from many.

Some brave men post up near the edge and chat with us. It's innocent at first, then the charming smiles begin to disappear, and the jokes become dirtier and dirtier.

"Say, *we here* recruitin' pretty girls to ride out the hurricane at our crib. We got drinks, drugs, a refrigerator full of food, a generator, and boxes of rubbers."

His partner adds, "It's gon' be a good time. What

better way to spend being stuck inside while nature does its thing?"

Sonya speaks for the both of us. "Sir, you and your friend are excused."

"Figures," says the ugly one. "Boujee-ass bitches think y'all special 'cause y'all sittin' in VIP."

I turn to Sonya, and we laugh until they walk off.

She shakes her head. "If it wasn't for the word bitch, what would they have?"

"Absolutely nothing." I snicker. "And just like that, I'm back in the cesspool filled with pee."

I search in the darkness and strobe-lit crowd for familiar faces—one in particular, to be exact.

My eyes don't lock with anyone as I wait for my turn to be called to the stage, and I consume only one fruity drink so that my head is clear when it's time to go up. The shot I took with the owner, and the sex on the beach concoction is enough to remove my being on edge, in fear I'll see Coop's face in the crowd and ruin my set.

The emcee calls my name.

Sonya rubs my shoulder. "Bring down the house."

"I'll try. Tonight's poem is a bit different."

Sonya whistles as I walk to the stage. I laugh to myself, thinking of what my grandmother used to say about a whistling woman—*she ain't to be fucked with.* And that is true about my big sister.

My face holds a smile from the laugh as I grab the microphone. "Somebody said y'all was looking for me?" I give the crowd a humorous scowl.

They respond as a unit. "Here I go!"

We vibe together as a collective once the deejay plays the instrumental to the quoted Mystikal song. I do a little shimmy to the beat then signal for the deejay to cut the tune short.

"Y'all ready!" I say to the hyped crowd, settling my nerves. "I better not disappoint tonight, then, huh." I adjust the microphone. "Ooh. The pressure. Speaking of pressure, ladies, have you ever had to regroup before you lose yourself? You see."

I run my mouth a lot but this man knows how to pacify
(I smirk at the audience getting what I'm putting down)
Then it be nice and slick when he pulls it out and reach for my
Pleasure palace, punani, pussy whatever you wanna call it—
waiting to be electrified
And when I feel him inch by inch by inch slip inside
Mmm, I always sigh

I gotta catch my breath with that one
Pure satisfaction
Never turn down his action
But he gotta catch me too cause I'm a fast one

Just cause he got that good good and I like it, it ain't taming me
He got game but not more game than me
Cause I'll move around shamelessly
I know my worth and let you know it ain't no shame in me
Thick and wide hipped is my claim to be
Shit, a smart motherfucker would put a claim in me
If you get whipped don't go blaming me
Cause you ain't gon' find nothing wetter than the lane in me

Mmmm that's my delight
If it's wrong it feels right

My legs bent over his shoulder
As he digs into me over and over and over
Pause mid stroke, pulls it out and goes lower
(I exhale)
Tastes the oil he's plowed from my goldmine
Re-lubing my wall like a paint roller
Serving as the placeholder in my folder
While my sun powers his battery, call me Solar

I'm pressure baby.

I step back from the microphone. The women stand and give me applause. I take a bow and thank the crowd with praying hands as I walk offstage, greeted with shoulder rubs, praises, respect nods, and random shouts of, "Pressure baby!" and "Talk yo' shit, girl!" said to me until I reach my table.

"Sis! You killed that!"

Sonya's approval makes me blush.

I say to her, "This is the part I'm not comfortable with."

"What?"

"The stares and compliments. It's a weird feeling. I like that people like my poetry, but this part makes me want to go into hiding. You ready?"

She slurps the last drop of her cocktail. "Sure. It's getting too hot in here anyway."

She leads us through the overcrowded floor covered in spilled drinks, paper cups, and sticky residue. My head faces down as I walk behind her, glued to her heels, thanking those who share with me that they loved my performance.

It's muggy outside, but the heat outdoors is better than the different smells from assorted bodies of heat inside the lounge.

"Imagine that," I say, fanning my chest with my shirt when we reach the exit.

"What?"

"Saying the dry heat outside feels good."

"Innit." She fans herself.

"Milena." Leo cuts in front of me.

"I know you fuckin' lying." Sonya steps forward with bloodshot eyes.

I hold her back with my arm.

Leo scoffs at her. "Can I talk to you for a second?" he asks me.

"We don't have anything to talk about."

Sonya pulls me. "Not a damn thing. Let's go."

"Milena, I only need…"

"To thank me! You got what you wanted! You get nothin' else!"

Sonya and I walk away before the alcohol she's consumed leads to a bad decision that will put her in the backseat of a Ford with swollen wrists.

When we get in the car, Sonya holds my hand. "I'm proud of you. You hear me. You alright?"

"I'm good. I just want the past to stay in the past."

Ding. Both of our phones chime with a text message in our group chat with Ma.

Drunk monks,
Hurricane Caprice is now a category 5. We are leaving
first thing in the morning. Sober up!

Two hours of packing, five hours of sleep, and eight hours of a road trip fueled on coffee, water, and fear, we hit the road out of South Carolina.

"Thank God it's only three of us in the car," Ma fusses. "You two don't know how to pack light."

"Ma, you've literally scared us about how bad this

storm is gonna be, as if we haven't been through a hurricane before."

"Yeah, but you two didn't survive Hugo, and this one got all the makings just like that monster. Three weeks of no power in the worst heat will never escape my memory. I'd rather put up with my sister's shit for a few weeks than live through searching for water to flush my toilet. My God, I never sweated so much in my life. Just you two watch. When the helicopters fly over the aftermath, and the news shows the world what Charleston looks like when Caprice has blown over, y'all two are gonna be thankful we left."

"We might be gone three weeks, and you're spazzing out about the few bags we packed. I only brought my most prized possessions, music, books, and clothes."

"Chile, I packed one week of clothing, my photo albums, and my jewelry. One load of clothing to be washed is all it takes to survive."

"Yeah, if you ain't going to the clubs—which is where I'll be."

"Ain't nothing in the club but whores, man-whores, pushers, pimps, and lost folk. I'll be glad when you realize that. *You done* came home and got your sister hooked up in that mess."

Sonya adds, "I don't go with her all the time."

"You used to not go at all." Her eyes shoot daggers at me through the rearview mirror. "And I thought you were seeing someone. What could be in the club when you got someone to spend time with."

"Ma, we got a long drive ahead of us. Is this how you want to start it off?"

She sucks her teeth. "I never did have control over you—or that tongue of yours."

"This tongue has never disrespected you."

She mutters. "Not to my face."

Sonya and I snicker.

"I know you two talk about me when I ain't 'round."

"Actually, we don't. Why are you so riled up?"

She takes a deep sigh. "'Cause *we in* this traffic, assholes are on the road, and I thought if we left early, we'd avoid all of this."

"Looks like everyone had the same idea as you."

"Umph, umph, umph. Can't blame people for being smart. I'm telling you, before Hugo hit, the sky turned all colors of the rainbow. People claimed clouds shaped like Jesus appeared in the sky. And a gloom hit the city before it arrived, creating panic. The police had to shut down *the I* coming into Charleston and reverse traffic so folks could escape." Her mouth falls flat into a line. "This storm feels a lot like ole Hellraiser Hugo."

I press on the gas as the traffic lets up. "Thank God for coffee, 'cause I don't wanna experience no parts of that."

Sonya looks back at Ma. "I'm praying we have a house to come back home to."

"Amen."

The car silences, and my mind immediately goes back to the slick dig Ma made about heauxs being in the club. Ever since she learned about my fling with Leo in high school, she's thought of me as loose. Sometimes I wondered if I played into the way she thought about me. Sometimes I accepted freedom of my body autonomy made her assumptions true. Either way, I had no problem living my life out loud, the way I wanted to.

But when the two of them made the comment about home, I felt that gloom Ma described shadowing the city cover me like a blanket. They spoke of our family house as their own—*their* home. And though I would always be welcome, it was a house full of memories that would one day be passed down to Sonya, not me. *I need a place to call my own.*

As I weave in and out of lighter traffic, thinking about the idea of home and what it means, Coop's face lingers in my thoughts. Ma asking about him surprised me and freed him from the corner of my mind where I pretended I could forget about him. It was as if she knew I was hiding a broken heart and forcing me to face my truth.

For miles and miles along the stretch of crowded roads beneath a gray sky, his face keeps me company, occupying my thoughts like a tenant. But the farther I drive out of the city, the pain I've been holding onto lifts. Out of sight and out of mind, making it easier to move on from what we could have been.

CHAPTER 29

COOP

Catastrophic. The news describes the hurricane as deadly. Essential employees are required to be on standby, and I'm grateful my position as a lead isn't included in that chain.

A company-wide email grants us early dismissal to prepare for the inevitable, and personnel rush out of the office to join the flooded roads of traffic, slammed together like a scene in an apocalyptic movie.

Bypassing over 26, the highway is already jam packed by those getting the early start to evacuate. But like the other times we've faced torrential storms, I post up at my mother's house nearby in Ladson.

Before the hurricane blows through Holy City, I type *'Call me'* to Milena, backspace those words, re-type *'Call me if you need anything'*, then delete that message completely as pride overcomes me. I'm not ready to accept she'll be partying and sexing some new bozo in the desert, and the more I think about it, the more a bad taste forms in my mouth.

'I'm not the one in the wrong. She should reach out to me first.'

I unpack what I deem of value into my old room then make it back to the kitchen to unpack the groceries I was able to score from the nearly empty shelves. As I put away all the ingredients for the coffee blend I've become addicted to, Ma Dukes walks in.

She takes the carton from my hand. "Whatchu know about flavored creams?"

My face drops as I figure out how to explain myself. I realize Mimi may not be around physically, but parts of her will be forever, especially when it comes to taste.

I catch myself slipping and answer, "Want me to show you?"

"In the morning, if we haven't lost power yet. If I drink coffee right now, I'll be up all night."

"I'll have it ready for you when you wake up."

She playfully sings. "Breakfast in bed too?"

"Anything for you, Mama." I kiss her cheek.

"You talk to your daddy?"

"I saw him last night."

"Good. He told me you two are at odds. I said to him, "What kind of man argues with his son?" I can't recall a time y'all ever had a falling out."

"There's a first time for everything, I guess."

Her eyes pierce into mine. "Well, y'all fixed it is all that matters."

I shy away. "I'm gonna board up the windows and bring the generator inside just in case it floods."

I escape her prying, knowing my old man didn't say shit about why we were arguing, the same way he didn't speak up when he should have. I won't be the one to make my mother relive the lies and games he played with her or bring up their past that I'm not sure she ever got over, though I'm curious how much she knows.

'Does she know about Melina? Have they ever met? Does she know she's the reason me and Pop are at odds?'

As promised, I fix my famous pancakes and hash browns in the morning. The smell of Melina's special blend lights up the house, and Ma calls me from her bedroom.

"What you got going on in there?!"

"You stay off your feet. I'm bringing it to you now."

She slices the flapjacks into squares and triangles, closes her eyes when she takes the first bite, then sips the coffee.

She scoffs. "Tell me...you've been hanging out in them swanky, overpriced coffee joints popping up everywhere or something?" She takes a second sip. "Making coffee like this, you've been hanging somewhere."

"No, ma'am. I bought a cookbook," I *sorta* lie. "Why? You like it?"

"I might want this every morning." She slurps from the mug. "I hear the winds have picked up."

"Yeah. The outer bands are rolling in. That's why I came yesterday. I didn't wanna risk being caught out there, trying to get to you in case the storm picked up speed."

"I'm sure grateful for a good son." Her hand cups my cheek. "I might have wasted my youth on your daddy, but it gave me you. That's the only reason I'm able to forgive him. Well...you and the Lord."

"God is good."

"All the time." She lifts another square to her mouth. "And I'm gon' take that as you wanna go to church with me on Sunday."

"Let's make it through the storm before you get me to making promises."

✳

By nightfall, we're in the dark. I turn on a few battery-powered LED lights and sit quietly with my phone in my hand. Rain is being dumped on the house like a ship in the middle of the Atlantic. Winds are whistling and shaking the house as if the bricks aren't strong enough to withstand its gusts.

The outer bands have intensified and blow like the Big Bad Wolf, beating against the wood. My mother's house holds up like the last little pig in the fairy tale, but the sounds of God's fury outside frightens her out of her bed.

She joins me in the living room. "Did I sleep through the eye?"

"You did. The front was not as bad as the tail."

"How's your father holding up?"

"I have no idea. I'm saving my battery in case we have an emergency."

"Checking on your daddy ain't gon' kill your battery. Call him."

I dial the old man.

"Everything okay?!" he yells on the line when he answers.

"So far, so good," I mumble.

My mother smiles. She knew I was still pissed with him when we talked earlier. I imagine she knew she would use the storm to make us mend fences.

"Ma wants to know how you're holding up?"

"Maintainin', but I tell ya, the sounds I'm hearin' ain't assurin'."

"Well, let's save our batteries. Call us when it's over."

"10-4."

I hang up the line. "Did that make you happy?"

"It did." She grabs one of the lights from the table. "I'm gonna go read my Bible now."

It's still dark outside when the storm passes. At first light, I attempt to go outside and assess the damage.

Trees are stuck in roofs, water is as high as the porch, and power lines drape across cars.

I swish through water half a foot high to remove the boarded wood from the front window.

Mr. Jim, the HOA president, floats by on a kayak. "Everyone okay over here?"

"We made it through. How about your family?"

"Everyone's fine. Damn *churn* already complaining it ain't no Wi-Fi."

I chuckle. "I didn't think about that."

"Well, I'm making the rounds to see how everyone made out and to remind you not to fire up a generator if you have one until the water recedes."

"Noted."

"And don't walk through this water. Gators are gonna be on the prowl."

"Yes, sir."

The damage is horrific, comparable to a dystopian film. The scene reminds me how important it is to have someone to love through dark times. I go back inside, swallow my pride, and use what's left of my battery to message Mimi.

> 'I hope you're okay. Seeing the
> aftermath this morning has given me
> clarity. We started over once before.
> Maybe we can try again. Call me
> when you get this. There's something
> I need to tell you.'

The buzzing of saws powering up outweighs the neighbors crying in the windows of their homes. I assume they are tears of joy that we survived, or tears of fright at the sight of debris, trees, garbage, and outside furniture trapping us like lab rats.

Mama wakes up and stands next to me, looking

out from my bedroom window. She sees the neighborhood is in shambles and holds onto my arm.

"If it looks like this up here, I can only imagine how it looks downtown."

"Maybe gentrification is a curse." I shrug my shoulders.

Ma taps my arm. "Jermaine."

"I'm just saying. I know you've heard hurricanes are created from the spirit of African women thrown overboard during slavery."

"Boy, if you don't stop that talk. Where did you get that from?"

"I don't know. Around. But you don't ever have to worry about me disrespecting no woman. I want no part of y'all's vengeance."

I stay with Ma for over a week, until the water dries up and her power is restored. How we survived without a fan and no air conditioner in the dry heat will forever be a mystery.

Two weeks after the storm has delivered us into the past, the office passes inspection and is deemed safe for working conditions. One by one, my team returns.

Sage swings by my office. "Hey. You survived."

I push back in my chair. "I did. But next time, I'm gonna do what you did." I tap my pen against the desk. "Y'all have fun out west?"

"We did." She smiles. "We did worry about the people left behind whenever we saw the news, but for the most part, it was nice."

"How's Mimi?"

Her face dims. "Good. Her mother and sister are on their way back now."

"From where?"

"Virginia. They stayed with family in Arlington, I believe."

"Oh. I thought Milena went with you, but since she hasn't returned my message inquiring if she was okay, I began to worry she was here somewhere without power." If I could turn red, it would be now of embarrassment for prying.

Sage twists and looks away. "I thought she would have called you by now."

"Me too." I inhale and hold it.

"I guess you'll find out soon enough."

"Find out what?"

"Milena's not coming back."

"What do you mean not coming back?"

"She's staying up there. Her uncles said that her mother's house is flooded, so she and Sonya are gonna live in Milena's apartment until the lease is up."

"When is she coming for her things?"

Sage shrugs. "She didn't say."

We both scowl at the uncomfortable silence.

"Sorry to be the one to tell ya." She folds her lips. "I'm gonna go catch up on my emails. Glad you're okay."

The news of Milena moving puts me in a sunken place. I skip going home after work and spend the evening at my mother's house. Her home cooking is better than take-out, and her love soothes my broken heart without her even knowing it.

"I don't know what's bothering you, but don't dwell on it too long. Time can't be bottled up."

I save face with a lie. "I'm fine, Ma. Just got some news I wasn't expecting today."

She places a plate of shrimp and grits smothered in gravy in front of me. My comfort meal. Then, she stares at me with tight-pressed lips and her arms folded. She doesn't buy my story.

CHAPTER 30

MIMI

I sigh. First at the idea that I'll live in the room above my cousin's garage until I find a job. A second time when Ma and Sonya drive to South Carolina without me.

I don't want to see the damage left behind—or the man I left on read. The man who asked me to call him, but I avoided doing so because hearing his voice would put me back at square one of moving on without him.

Everyone around claims to have the hook-up on a government job that begins with a thick application with the OPM and loads of interviews and testing—a process I can't wait around for living with a nosey cousin that quizzes me about my daily Metro travels and how the job search is coming as soon as she walks into her house.

One week of the loud hint that I am overstaying my welcome, I dig into my savings, buy two pairs of black pants and six blouses, and settle for a substitute teaching position that surprisingly pays the same as Sonya's salary.

I work in the education system for a good month when they offer me a position to cover for a teacher on a long-term leave of absence. I accept then move into a fully furnished studio apartment fifteen miles away from the school.

The club scene becomes non-existent, riding public transportation. And without Sonya or Sage at my side, so has the desire to go. *'Mama put mouth on me. I just know it.'*

I haven't flirted, dated, hooked up, or swiped since I've arrived. Something is different about me here. I wonder if it's the distance or because it's the first time I've lived out of state.

The noticeable change in the temperature before the sun sets and how cold it is the closer Thanksgiving approaches takes some getting used to. Back home, I could still wear a short-sleeve shirt to fight the crowds on Black Friday. But up here, I'm forced to buy a few sweaters before the holiday sales begin as I put off returning home to collect my belongings.

School lets out on Tuesday before Turkey Day. The librarian, Tisa, who I've been friendly with, invites me over to her house since I slipped that I'm single and live alone.

"I want you to meet my brother, Jarvis. I think you two would get on," she says.

"Maybe when I get back." I rush for the door. "I'm on the first train to South Carolina in the morning."

"Oh. Well. Happy Thanksgiving. See you when you get back."

"Yeah. You too."

I hurry to catch the bus to my apartment, wondering if Tisa's brother looks like her. *Is he as talkative? Attractive? Can he hold a candle to Coop?*

⁂

I snuggle under a blanket for the first few hours of travel, and peel from under it the closer the rail arrives in The Carolinas. Sonya picks me up, and a sadness fills me, thinking of romantic movies where the heroine's love interest greets her coming off the train.

"It's good to see you too." Sonya shoves me.

"Thanks for coming to get me. *You ready* to share a bed with me?"

"For how long?" She jokes. "If big-city life isn't what you thought it'd be, just say so. I don't know what made you wanna stay anyway."

I turn up my lip. "I think you do."

She nods and places her arm around me. "Yeah, I do. You gonna call him?"

"Nope. I'm actually set to meet someone when I get back. My first date since the breakup."

"Good for you. Maybe the pool isn't full of pee up there."

"We'll see."

Day one, Sage catches me up with the latest gossip. Day two, I'm surrounded by family at my uncle's house in the country and a feast of Southern dishes I've been craving for weeks.

My cousins leave just before midnight to catch drunken women at the club. I sit this one out to drive Ma to the sales before daybreak. The grin on her face approves of my choice to not be out amongst the heauxs and hoods.

I sleep off the trip, the food, and the shopping Friday night, and join Sage and Sonya for brunch on Saturday then pack up my car to hit the road early Sunday morning.

"You really aren't going to see him?" Sage asks me.

I shake my head. "I'm being smart here. He would never choose me over his father, and I don't want to cause a rift between them."

"Rell and I went to open mic a few times. I saw Coop there once. I swear he was looking at the stage, hoping you would pop out."

"You know I haven't written a word since I've left."

"You have writer's block?"

"I have writer's block, cock block, fun block. You name it. I just need a reset."

"You can always come back, ya know."

"*Ihh.*" I exhale deeply. "Maybe one day. I don't know. I made a commitment to the school, and I'm kind of growing fond of the *churn*. Can you believe it?"

"I cannot."

"Like...I kind of see why Sonya is passionate about what she does. You grow attached to those little faces."

Sage glares at me. "Who are you?"

"That's a question I've been wrestling with myself."

❦

Tisa's brother, Jarvis, wants to meet midweek for drinks. I push for the weekend but give in to his hazel eyes and a picture of him with his shirt off on Instagram.

I enjoy a slamming crab dip while I wait for the five-foot-ten drummer to arrive. Twenty minutes late, he strolls in.

Right off the bat, I can tell his light-brown ass is full of himself—something I should have picked up on over the phone when he wouldn't budge to my suggestion of meeting on Friday night, a non-school night.

I've memorized the menu but pretend to read it while I wait for him to join me. He struts over in a cocky fashion and sits before saying hello—before acknowledging me by name.

I greet him. "Traffic?"

"Always."

"I'm Milena."

"Jarvis."

"Nice to meet you."

"Yeah. My sis thinks we'd get along."

I pause from his candor. "That's what she told me too." I watch his roaming eyes avoid mine. "So, I know you're a musician. Do you perform anywhere around here?"

"We play all over."

"Cool. I write as my creative outlet, but it's nothing I plan on pursuing." I hand him the menu. "I asked the waitress to wait to take our order."

He stares at the menu as if he's not impressed. But this is the place he chose to meet. How can he not know what he wants?

We sit in silence while he studies the options. I grow impatient. Impassive. Then, regret finds its way into my emotion for agreeing to this waste of time.

I take a deep breath and exhale. Hope erases the doubt and regret pushing my tongue to say something rude. I give him a few more seconds to make conversation then try to lighten the mood.

"Jarvis, darling," I tease him with a rolling, purring tongue. "Haven't you eaten here before?"

He looks up at me with a serious face.

I lean forward with raised brows. "Eartha Kitt?"

His expression remains blank.

"Thee Eartha Kitt. The legend," I say to him, smiling. "I wonder if I'm related to her sometimes. She's my spirit animal, and from my neck of the woods, it could be a possibility."

He's clueless to the reference. Unamused.

I sit back in my chair. "Tell me you've seen *Boomerang*?"

"I haven't."

"Really?" My voice softens. "I love watching the classics. Movies were better back in the day. More real and authentic. And Eddie Murphy is the GOAT."

"Can't say I've watched any classics." He places the menu on the table. "Excuse me for a second."

"Sure."

Jarvis walks over to the bar and signals for the bartender.

I hail for the waitress. "The gentleman I was waiting for is ordering himself a drink." I point to him chatting it up with some white girls giving him all of their attention.

Not one, but two strokes land on his arm. The waitress looks down on me.

My finger circles the basket of chips. "This is on him."

"I gotcha." She huffs and shakes her head.

I put on my coat, grab my bag, and take one final look at Jarvis, who's oblivious that I'm heading for the door. He's deep in the web of the two girls setting their trap while falling for him, and it tickles me. I pull out my phone and text Sonya.

'Not only is the pool full of pee. It's full of shit too. LOL TTYS'

CHAPTER 31

COOP

Sage slips that Mimi was in town. I'm speechless. Fuming. Hurt.

'She avoided me?'

We've had weeks to let the tension simmer, while the fire that burns between us is still very much alive, despite the cold winter. I feel it, though she's miles away. And she does too, I convince myself.

'It's why she couldn't face me.'

Distraught, I persuade Donald to grab our lunch to go while I raise hell in the car.

Barely touching my burger, I snap. "I would have at least stopped by to say hey. How you doing? Good to see ya. Something."

"She might have thought you had a chick over and didn't want to see that."

"She could have called."

"Perhaps," he says, bobbing his head. "But if she's trying to move on, do you think it's wise to be in your company so soon?"

"Are you suggesting I was right? That she's not over me?"

He shrugs. "It's obvious you ain't over her. Maybe the feeling is mutual. I don't know. Women are a species I'll never fully understand. And break-ups are tricky."

The idea that Milena isn't over me brings me comfort. I sit with it and take a bite of my sandwich that hits the spot above my stomach where it's churning in knots. My chest fills with rushed food traveling down my throat and anxiety of the unknown.

I swallow and confess. "I wrote her a poem."

Donald cackles loud over the music. "You did what?"

I laugh with him. "I wrote something besides a business proposal and TPS report."

He catches the joke from one of my favorite movies and loses it. "If you could just go ahead and do that," he chortles, quoting the famous line from *Office Space*.

I chime in. "That'd be great!"

"Peter Motherfuckin' Gibbons!" Donald hi-fives me. "But for real, though, in all seriousness, *you* wrote a *poem*? You some kinda, ugh, Andre 3000 haiku motherfucka or somethin' now?"

"Shut up." I lower my head, ashamed. "I think it came out good. I think she'd like it."

"Let me hear it."

I pull out the folded Post-it from my wallet, sip my soda, then clear my throat.

My heart is in duress, missing the slenderness of your tenderness.
The womanly way you pull what I push
I won't stop until my two hands caress your
sweet ass and my stick is back in your bush.
I miss the taste of your mouth keeping me warm this winter.
The taste of your juice flowing down like a blood orange sliced down the center.

"Whoa, whoa, whoa, man. You can't say that shit to her."

"Why not?"

"Because it's awful." He laughs hysterically. "What are you? A horny teenager dreaming about getting laid?"

"No, but she *do got* that Wi-Fi, D. I ain't never talked to you about my dealings like that, but Mimi got that hot spot. And she's sexy as fuck to me. Her mind is different from other girls. The way she walks, thinks, talks, performs...I just can't stop thinking about her."

"And what about the shit with your old man? I mean, she could have been your stepmother if things hadn't..."

I cut him short. "But she's not."

He holds up his hands. "Okay. Okay. Don't shoot the messenger. I'm just pointing out, will you be able to live with what took place in the past?"

"I can."

"Then tell her. I hope she feels the same." D pauses. "'Cause you've called that woman's name twenty-nine times today."

"Have I?"

"Yes! But do me a favor."

"Anything."

"Throw that poem away. It's one thing for a woman to recite such words. It's perverted when a man does. Write something from the heart, and leave the poetry to her."

⁂

"We've never been introduced. I'm Jermaine. Jermaine Cooper," I say, to a honey-toned woman that resembles Mimi but is decades older. "I'm Milena's friend."

"I gathered."

"Are you her sister?"

She grunts with a smile. "Her mother." Her eyes glance over me. "What business do you have with my daughter?"

I clear my throat. "You, actually. Sage mentioned you and Milena's sister took over her apartment after the storm. I should have come by sooner to check on you two, but..." I begin to stutter. "I honestly didn't know what to do."

"And now?"

"Now, I feel confident in saying I should have met you sooner—I wish I had met you sooner. And I need your advice."

"Come in. Have a seat."

Mrs. Reid welcomes me with open arms, having no knowledge of me at all. She reveals she knew Milena was seeing someone before she left. That she was content. And that Milena has never brought a man home to meet her family.

"You are the first young man I've ever had the pleasure of meeting that is interested in my daughter."

I stare at her in disbelief.

'The first? Is what happened with my father scarred her? Is this the missing piece of the Milena puzzle I've been dying to know? The explanation of her restraint? Her apprehension? Her hard shell?'

"I love your daughter. I never got the chance to tell her that, and I would like to do so face to face."

Her head shifts to the side. "Do you have any idea where she is?"

"Virginia, from what I'm told."

She sits up straight. "My daughter keeps her love life a secret from me. And it's nice to see she has a respectable gentleman such as yourself interested in her. But I feel compelled to tell you that long-distance relationships don't often work. And she's committed herself to a job for six months up there. So you think about that before you approach her." Her eyes narrow in on me. "I'd hate to be an accomplice to someone who is gonna waste her time."

"Yes, ma'am."

She goes to a desk covered with trinkets, mail, plates, and stacked picture frames. While she fumbles through papers, I look around at the extra pieces of furniture in the living room. The style and neatness that once graced the space is now buried and meshed with a second home. Victimized by the hurricane.

Mrs. Reid sits next to me. "Milena decided she wanted to have her first white Christmas this year. My brothers are driving the family up there to surprise her on Christmas Eve. You should know, my daughter is not fond of surprises, but if what you say is true—about loving her—she may make an exception for you." She hands me a piece of paper with Milena's address on it. "*And* you can do me a favor and give her a warning we're coming."

"Thank you." I hug Mrs. Reid. "For this." I squeeze the note. "For sitting with me. For the advice. For everything."

"You're welcome. And maybe I'll see you at Christmas."

Without making the conscious decision, I wind up at my father's house. I ring the bell, and he answers with a smile.

"Come on in."

"I'd rather stay out here."

The light in his face dims. "We good?"

"We'll see." I put my hands in my pockets. "I know I ain't mad at you anymore."

He scoffs. "Guess I got my hopes up too soon. Thought you stoppin' by meant you were ready to talk. For real this time. Like we used to do."

"I just came by to see if you were ready to answer that question."

"We've been through this, son."

"I need to know."

"Why is that question so important to you?"

"You first."

Pop steps down on the porch in his t-shirt and sweats. He leaves the front door cracked, but I still can hear the television in the living room.

We stand arm's length apart in the dropping temperature, blowing puffs toward each other, waiting for the other to speak first.

"I did." He looks me dead in the eyes. "As in the past. I did love her—or at least I thought I did. I just got confused when I saw her, ya know. It's been years, but the history is there, and to this very moment I don't know if there is a correct way I could have handled this." He takes a breath. "I said I was sorry. *It's* nothing more I can say."

"I'm going after her."

Pop breathes out through his nose.

"I came by here to tell you that. And if she'll have me, I need to know if we're gonna be okay?"

"Jermaine."

"'Cause if not, you'll still be my father, and I love you—but I choose her."

"Son."

"If you and her were meant to be, you would be. And what I need you to do is get over it and accept us. If you can't, tell me now."

"A billion people on the planet, son."

"And she's my person." I shrug.

"You won't feel awkward?"

"I've had time to think about this. And no. I won't. What happened between you two is in the past —and was wrong on so many levels. But me and her... feels right. If us being together is gonna make you feel awkward, then I'll keep my distance but still love you from afar until you come around."

He shivers and wells up with tears.

"I love you, Pop. You're my old man. But I love her too."

His head and shoulders drop.

"I'll give you time to think on it." I step away and head back to my car.

"Maine!"

I turn around.

He lifts his hand. "I love you, boy. You're *my* boy. And I'll always be here for you."

I meet him where he stands and shake his hand. "Thanks, Pop. Love you too."

⁂

Four days before Christmas, I send a single rose to Milena's apartment. Three days before Christmas, I send a half dozen roses with a card that reads, *A rose is still a rose.*

Two days before Christmas, I send a dozen roses to her place with a copy of the lyrics to the tune she was humming the day she extended the olive branch.

The delivery guy places them in front of her door and knocks. The door swings open, and she's as breathtaking as I remember her. Her hair is straight, swinging over her shoulder. Her plump, luscious legs shine in knit shorts that match a long-sleeve sweater hanging off the other shoulder.

She kneels to smell the arrangement. The note falls on the floor, and she picks it up. While she's reading it, I step into the hallway and recite the hook to her.

"Coffee in the morning?"

Milena's eyes meet mine. "How did you know I liked that song?"

I walk toward her. "You were humming it one day. I drove myself crazy until I found out the name of it."

She smiles at me.

"Is this a bad time?"

Her body twists side to side. "What are you doing all the way up here?"

"Taking a chance."

She folds the note, and her smile grows bigger. "I thought about something the other day."

I reach for her hand. "What's that?"

She places her hand in mine. "I never tasted your pancakes."

"I know the recipe by heart. You want them for dinner or breakfast?"

"I want them for breakfast. Many breakfasts."

I pull her close and take ownership of her lips. She falls into me. It feels like a heavy load is lifted from the both of us, and all's right with the world.

"It's a good thing I know the recipe by heart."

She laughs and rests her head on my chest.

"I added a special tweak to them too."

"Is that right?"

"I add a dollop of whipped cream on top. It doesn't taste as good as you—I mean yours—but I think you'll like it. Maybe even love it. The way I love you." I hold her face in my hands. "I love you, Mimi."

"I love you, Jermaine Cooper."

We fall into another lip lock filled with all the emotions we put on the back burner the past few months. I squeeze her tightly in my arms, happy to have the chance to hold her again.

She invites me inside. "You couldn't live without me, huh?"

"Tried to. I even wrote you a poem."

"Noooo," she drags a light laugh.

The door closes behind us. I press her against it

and stare into her eyes, holding them with mine, filled to the brim with joy like a child getting a new bike on Christmas morning. And it feels better than good to be on the other side with Milena Natasha Reid. My queen.

Dearest Reader

Please leave a review.

To the readers who found my story on the soon-to-be extinct app Kindle Vella, your likes, comments, and weekly faves will forever hold a special place in my heart. I hope you add this book to your shelf and know how much I am beyond grateful for the support you have shown me.

Thank you to Jenn Lockwood for editing this story, and thank you in advance to everyone that will leave a review on all the platforms, and spread the word about Heavy Whipped Cream.

 MBP

About the Author

Mahogany B. Preston is a North Charleston, S.C. native who loves plants, being outdoors, and learning new trades. She considers herself to be a professional student as she satisfies her curiosity by enrolling in free courses, no matter the subject.

As an emerging author whose body of work features romantic comedies, humorous holiday women's fiction, and witty novellas. Her specialty is banter, making her audience enjoy a chuckle or two.

Mahogany hopes that one day her love of knowledge will reveal the true secret of life. If she uncovers that mystery, she will then have to decide if she can share it.

This is Mahogany's first book. Please sign up for her newsletter and follow her on the featured social media platforms.

thembp.kit.com

Also by
Mahogany B. Preston

PANTY CLAUS

HEAVY WHIPPED CREAM IN PRINT

ARRIVES SPRING 2025